Squad

Squ

MARIAH MacCARTHY

FARRAR STRAUS GIROUX

NEW YORK

Farrar Straus Giroux Books for Young Readers
An imprint of Macmillan Publishing Group, LLC
175 Fifth Avenue, New York, NY 10010

1   3   5   7   9   10   8   6   4   2

fiercereads.com

Library of Congress Cataloging-in-Publication Data

Names: MacCarthy, Mariah, author.
Title: Squad / Mariah MacCarthy.
Description: First edition. | New York : Farrar Straus Giroux, 2019. |
    Summary: "High school cheerleader Jenna is slowly losing her best friend,
    Raejean, and the trust of her teammates after an incident at a party.
    Through miscommunication, misinterpretation, and retaliation, the world as
    she knows it crumbles around her"—Provided by publisher.
Identifiers: LCCN 2018020387 | ISBN 9780374307509 (hardcover)
Subjects: | CYAC: Cheerleading—Fiction. | Best friends—Fiction. |
    Friendship—Fiction. | High schools—Fiction. | Schools—Fiction.
Classification: LCC PZ7.1.M2443 Sq 2019 | DDC [Fic]—dc23
LC record available at https://lccn.loc.gov/2018020387

Our books may be purchased in bulk for promotional, educational, or business use. Please
contact your local bookseller or the Macmillan Corporate and Premium Sales Department at
(800) 221-7945 ext. 5442 or by email at MacmillanSpecialMarkets@macmillan.com.

For Leo, always.

one

I JUST WOKE UP ONE MORNING AND FORGOT HOW to do everything. I didn't have a stroke, or an accident, or get diagnosed with a disability; it's just that one moment everything was easy, and the next it wasn't.

I'm Jenna Watson, and I'm a cheerleader. I know, I know. But it's not some Hollywood crap, okay? We are not every guy's fantasy; we are not the "popular girls" or the "mean girls" of Marsen High School. We're too busy for that. We're literally just some human females trying to live our lives and do a perfect toe touch.

Because here's something very important for you to understand: Cheerleading is a sport. I know, I know. But listen: *Cheerleading is a sport, damn it.* We get up at the butt crack of dawn, and we practice. We run laps and we drill and we jump up in the air over and over and over. We watch TV with our legs spread-eagle to maintain our flexibility even when we're "relaxing." We go to sleep with our fingers and toes twitching in rhythm as we run through our routines in our minds. We are athletes. And our team is at the top of its game. We've advanced to the state championship every year for the past decade, and made it to Nationals three of those years. We are serious.

I'm good. I'm a good cheerleader. Okay, I'm great. You can't be on the team if you're not great. I'm not the best one; I'm maybe the third best, though I might be tied with one or two other people for that slot. And that's fine. I don't need to be the best; I mean, I'm only a junior, so I'm still working on my form.

I'm also an A student, though I occasionally get the rogue B+. I'm fine with that, too, though I'm sure my mom would like me and my brother, Jack, to get straight As. Jack, by the way, is a Goth and a senior and weird, and he gets slightly more Bs than me, but we're both good students. We have a car that we share, though I use it more than him. And Dad is in absentia in Colorado with his younger hippie-granola wife I still haven't met, so Mom's been living that #singlemomlife the past six years—all of which just adds to the pressure for me to do well as a student and cheerleader. Fortunately, I am fantastic at both; you're welcome, Mom. I'm in good shape to get financial aid or a cheerleading scholarship from a university within a six-hour drive of where I live in San Diego, and that's basically what I'm going for.

So, that's my life. School, cheer practice, and the cheer *team*, which is its own commitment. The cheer girls are basically family. Like, you have to be, when you spend so much time up in each other's business. So when we're not at practice or games or on the road for competitions, we're usually at each other's houses or seeing a movie together or at the mall. We get our periods at the same time, we text constantly, we're always in each other's photos online—you get the picture.

Or that's how it was before I woke up and forgot how to do everything.

Okay, I didn't forget how to do *everything*. I could still ace an AP English test; I remembered all the moves to our routines; I could breathe and eat and walk around and stuff. I just forgot how to act like a normal person. And I'm not even sure if I forgot, or if the rules just changed on me. The first person I noticed it with was Raejean.

Raejean *was* my best friend, but things have been weird since we started junior year. We didn't have a fight or anything, more of an . . . incident, I guess. I don't even know if I'm the one being weird or if she is or we both are. I'm pretty sure it started at Billy's birthday party, though.

A little background: Billy Nguyen is cute as hell. He does the student announcements on campus TV in the morning, he's a little bit dorky, but he's adorable, and I'm not the only one who thinks so. He used to be a child model or something? We went to elementary and middle school together, but I just started crushing on him at the end of sophomore year after dumping my first real boyfriend, Roland Jackson.

Billy's birthday is September 10, so he always has a party right after the school year starts—I've been going to his birthday party every year since I was, like, seven. His house has a pool, so he had a pool party in the middle of the day on a Saturday. By the time it got dark, the last eight or nine of us—Raejean, me, Meghan and Becca from cheer, some other kids from our year—had abandoned the pool and piled into his living room to watch this stand-up routine that his friend Chris said we "just *had* to watch." I'd wanted to sit next to Billy on the couch, but this girl from my English class, Alison Boyer, sat by him instead, so I sat with Raejean on the floor.

I should clarify that Raejean wasn't in her bathing suit anymore. She'd changed back into this bright yellow sundress; not everyone can pull off yellow, but she can.

Oh, also, I was drinking a glass of water.

After watching the stand-up, we all just sat on the floor, giggling and quoting our favorite lines. "Oh my God, and the part about the ducks? Oh my God," I remember saying.

Raejean looked over at me and laughed. "Oh my God," she said, imitating me. "You are such a ditz."

It wasn't the first time she had called me a ditz, actually. She would call me a ditz when I was confused or said something in a particularly high vocal register. But for some reason, this time especially pissed me off. I'm not a ditz. I've never gotten below a B+ on *anything*. I'm not shallow; I'm not even blond like Raejean—not like it's cool to hate on blondes, either, but at least that would sorta make sense. I knew she was joking, but . . . I mean, what kind of joke is that? It's not even funny. What's the punch line supposed to be? Also, we're both cheerleaders! Don't we deal with enough "ditz" stereotypes already?

Maybe it's because I like Billy, and she knew I liked him. Maybe it's because she did it in front of a room full of people, instead of when it was just the two of us. But I could feel my face flushing. (I hate blushing. It's like strapping a big neon sign to my face that says EMBARRASSING THINGS ARE HAPPENING.)

So I did the first thing that came to mind: I dumped my glass of water over her head.

I don't remember how the room reacted. I think someone (maybe Chris?) went "Ohhhh!" like guys do. But what I mostly remember is the look of disgust and confusion and betrayal on Raejean's face. My decision to pour the water on her hung in the air like a bad smell. Immediately I wanted to take it back.

"Are you okay?" I found myself saying.

"What the hell is wrong with you?" she responded.

I felt like it shouldn't be such a big deal. Weren't we all just swimming two hours ago? It's *water*; it's not like it's gonna stain her clothes or anything. But I could tell it was a big deal.

"I'm sorry," I said, and then I was mad at myself for saying it. Why should I be sorry? She's the one always calling me a ditz for no reason!

I grabbed my towel and tried to help her dry off, but it was already wet from having used it after swimming, and she waved me away with her hands. The rest of the room had moved on to discussing a different part of the comedy routine, so I thought maybe all was forgotten, but no one really talked to me for the rest of the party. Then again, I didn't make an effort to talk to any of them, either. I just sat there, feeling my hot face burning a hole in the room, trying to disappear into the floor.

After all that, I had to give Raejean a ride home because we'd come to the party together. We didn't say anything in the car. I had music on, but I don't think that was why. She got out with a clipped "Seeya," and that was that.

Now it's nearly October, and things are still weird. It's not like she flat-out *ignored* me after that. I mean, she couldn't. But we kind of avoid eye contact, she just sends back one-word replies to my texts, and she's been getting rides home with Meghan Finnegan instead of with me. We also, for the first time, don't have any classes together this year; I'm in AP English, she's in Advanced, and they're different periods, which threw off all the rest of the classes we wanted to take with each other. So that's not helping, either.

This probably doesn't sound that bad. I don't know; maybe it's not. But this is the longest we've ever gone without going over to each other's house. Raejean has been my best friend since fourth grade. Raejean calls my mom "Mom." Raejean has slept in my bed with me hundreds or maybe thousands of times. Raejean can tell when I need to eat. If me and Raejean aren't okay, then the foundation of my world is cracked and crooked.

I wrote and deleted maybe a dozen e-mails, which basically went like this:

Hey girl. I'm just writing to say I hope things are cool with us.

I love you so much and I know it was totally weird that I dumped my water on you at Billy's party. I don't know why but being called a ditz right then just rubbed me the wrong way, and I totally overreacted. I'm super sorry and I hope you're not mad. Forgive me? I'll buy you a pumpkin spice latte?

(Raejean loses her shit for pumpkin spice lattes.)

Or maybe this is all in my head and you're actually not pissed at all? I feel like maybe I'm losing it because I can't stop thinking about this and I can't tell if I'm making this weird and things are fine, or if things are actually weird. Let a girl know. I love you boo.

I never e-mailed her. It felt too needy.

That was just the beginning of not knowing how to do anything anymore. A week after the water incident, while putting our clothes on after cheer practice, Meghan Finnegan was suddenly looking at my jeans a little too closely. Meghan's white and redheaded and *loud*, and everyone loves her, me included; she's not of Raejean-level importance to me, but she's probably the funniest person on the team. She poked me in the side, her eyes firmly on my crotch.

"Jenna, are we rocking a little camel toe?"

I blinked. "What?"

"You totally are! You've got some camel toe going on!"

"What's a camel toe?"

"You've never heard of camel toe?" She was laughing, her eyes were sparkling; it wasn't *mean*, but I could feel my face getting hot.

"No," I said. "What is that?"

"Becca," she called out. "Becca, come look at this! Does Jenna have some camel toe in these jeans?"

I'd worn this exact pair of jeans all the time. I couldn't figure out what could possibly be different right now.

Becca Ruiz looked at my crotch. "Oh my God, you totally do. You gotta retire those jeans, girl."

And suddenly Raejean was in on it, too. "Jenna!" she laughed. "I told you to get rid of those jeans!" No, actually, you never did, Raejean. You've told me repeatedly how cute you think I look in them . . .

What the hell is a camel toe? My voice wavered just a little bit, and this pissed me off even more, because it didn't seem like anything involving my jeans could be such a big deal.

"It means we can read your lips," said Meghan, laughing harder.

"Google it," said Becca. "And get some new jeans!"

I waited until later to google it, because I didn't want to give them the satisfaction of watching me standing there with my phone, discovering it in front of them. And I'm glad I waited, because I'm pretty sure my whole head turned bright red when I read the definition.

I mean, what the hell? I wore those jeans *all the time*. I hadn't gained weight. Why were they suddenly not okay?

It started to feel like something like this happened every day: some joke I wasn't in on, some social faux pas. "Um, did you just say *chillax*? What is this, the nineties?" "How can you still listen to that song after everyone and their mother has played it into the ground?" "Jenna, what's up with that lip gloss? Did you go down on Bert from *Sesame Street*?" As far as I could tell, it was just me. No one else was getting taunted for these kinds of missteps.

I couldn't figure it out. These girls were my *family*. We joked all the time that we were a hive mind, that we all had a psychic connection with one another. Why was I suddenly always a step behind?

two

WE'RE AT PRACTICE, AND COACH MASON IS singling out Raejean.

"Your legs are too straight coming out of the tuck jump," Coach says. "You're going to hurt yourself."

A tuck jump is basic, baaaasic cheerleading. "You can't slack off on the basics and save it all for the stunts," Coach says. "Every single move needs to be sharp and tight."

I am remembering fifth-grade figure skating lessons with Raejean; I am remembering Mrs. Rabinowitz, who thought the sun shone out of Raejean's fifth-grade ass; and I am remembering Mrs. Rabinowitz's successor, Kate Ross, who criticized Raejean's spirals. I am remembering how quickly after that Raejean decided that figure skating was for losers; I don't think she and Kate Ross lasted a month together.

Please, Raejean, don't fall out of love with cheerleading. Please don't leave me.

"Do it again," Coach says, and she makes Raejean do it alone. And then again. And then she puts her hands on Raejean, pushing her body down so her knees bend, demanding that we all watch.

We get notes all the time. It's how we've stayed at the top of our game for so long. But no one else is getting notes today, just Raejean.

Coach Mason is built like an SUV (indestructible) and makes you feel safe for the exact same reason. Her skin looks like a potato from too many suntans, and she is unapologetically demanding. Most days we are happy to sweat it all out on the mat for her, even when we complain in the locker room afterward, but this is a lot, even for Coach.

We all do the sequence again. "Good, Jenna." No no no. What are you doing? I don't want to be the good one; I don't want to be the example. I try to catch Raejean's eye to communicate all this, but her eyes are on herself in the mirror, jumping over and over and over again and making sure to bend her knees deeply on every landing. I look back at my reflection, and my face is pink. It's not my usual exertion pink. I know the difference.

Coach lays into Raejean through the whole practice. "Point that toe, Raejean." "Spine straight." "You're not moving with the group." "Get that leg up." I beg her in my mind to back off, but she just keeps going.

I put a hand on Raejean's bicep in the locker room after. "Coach is high," I say. "I don't know what crawled up her ass and died."

And Raejean doesn't even look at me as she shrugs. "She's just doing her job," she says.

"Yeah, but that was like . . . excessive."

She shrugs. Again. Still not looking at me. "Your aerials look good. You've been practicing."

It's dressed like a compliment, but she's not looking at me and she's shouldering her backpack and she's walking out without waiting for me, and when I come outside, I see her getting into Meghan's car.

I open up her name in my phone and tap out a text:

DON'T YOU DARE GHOST ON ME!!!

I stare at it, ashamed. It's clingy, it's desperate, it's terrifying. I decide not to send it.

Then somehow my thumb is pressing Send anyway. No no no nooooooo, take it back take it back, but there the notification is: **Delivered**. And then, almost immediately: **Read**.

I wait for the ellipsis on her end that will tell me she's typing back. It doesn't come.

Oh God oh God, what is happening. What did I do?

I type again.

Sorry. Meant to send that to someone else.

No, that's stupid, that's utterly transparent, she'll laugh at you. Delete, delete, delete, keep hitting Delete even though all the text is gone.

I'm standing in the parking lot; the squad has pretty much scattered. I look around and take a big breath. It's a sunny day, and I feel like I'm dying.

My phone buzzes. Text from Raejean:

???

I decide not to answer. I put my phone in my pocket. Then I take it back out and start typing.

Sorry. Got pissed for a minute—

Nope. Delete. I type again.

Nvm

Send.

Big breath, big breath, don't cry in the parking lot.

I suddenly do the math and realize it's been just three weeks since Billy's birthday party. It feels like it's been months and months. Three weeks is such a long time for me and Raejean not to be at each other's houses or staying up texting every night. Since Billy's birthday we've seen each other almost every day and said almost nothing.

I type another text:

Sleepover sometime? Been a minute

She writes back almost immediately:

Maybe after this weekend. Mrs. H assigned a ridic 8pg paper for Mon

Me: **OK. Or you can work on it at my place if you want. Miss u**

I waver before hitting Send; I don't know if the last sentence is too much, but since when do I worry about being "too much" with Raejean? Send.

Buzz.

OK I'll let u know.

I want to set myself on fire.

I crank my music in the car. Angry white boys with electric guitars. It doesn't help.

When I get home, I make a run for the cupboard and start shoving Reese's Puffs in my mouth like I'm starving. I close the cupboard door, and there's my brother, Jack, staring at me with his bored, eyelinered eyes.

"What are you doing?" he says.

"I'm . . . eating." I thought that much would be clear.

It's seventy degrees outside, but Jack is wearing black from head to toe, per usual. Black Pink Floyd T-shirt, black skinny jeans, black Converse sneakers. He used to wear black lipstick, but he said it chapped his lips too much; I asked him what brand he was using and offered to give him tips on keeping his lips moisturized, but he was over it by that point.

"I thought you didn't eat sugar."

This is true. I have mostly sworn off sugar since I joined cheer, with exceptions for special occasions. Coach hands out meal plans and recipe books to all the girls, which are "not mandatory, but which other girls have found useful," but you're basically not going to survive cheer if you keep eating Wendy's and Pop-Tarts all the time. Lots of hard-boiled eggs, green smoothies, and coconut oil. Very few Reese's Puffs.

"I'm hungry," I respond.

"That's my cereal."

"So have Mom get more."

"She doesn't go to the grocery store until Saturday."

"So get more yourself," I practically yell, and I flounce into my bedroom with the box of Reese's Puffs and slam the door.

Jack was my best friend before Raejean was my best friend. My mom loves to tell the story of how when I was three, some other kid at a park kept stealing my Teenage Mutant Ninja Turtles action figures, and Jack got right in that kid's face and bellowed, "*Don't. Do. That.*" The kid apparently ran away terrified.

When Dad left Mom six years ago for Renee (who is twenty-eight and posts farmers' market pictures on Instagram and who I still haven't met), I was ten and Jack was eleven. Jack scribbled *I hate Dad* all over the walls, and I helped him paint over it before Mom found out; we would camp out in each other's rooms, re-counting the latest fight we'd overheard. Raejean was my best friend by that point, and sometimes I'd cry to her at lunch or after figure skating practice, but I'd cry to Jack, too.

But then Jack started middle school and began painting his fingernails black and listening to Marilyn Manson, and I was taking dance and gymnastics classes, and he started judging everything I did. "Why are you listening to Kesha?" he'd ask. "She's so *boring*." He found other kids who wore black, and I started middle school and found other girls who liked Kesha, and that was kind of that.

Jack's room is illuminated only by a black light and whatever sunlight his curtains don't block out, the scent of incense wafting into the hallway whenever he opens his door. My room is peaceful, a little castle. The walls are lavender, and I've got a snow-white down comforter that makes me feel luxurious, something I had to beg Mom to get me for two consecutive years. The cheer trophies, the photos, the Lady Gaga poster are all scientifically placed and generally make me feel pretty Zen when I'm in here.

Today I just keep thinking about all the sleepovers I haven't been having with Raejean lately, and it feels like jail.

I'm sitting on my bed, shoveling dry cereal, staring at my phone screen, scrolling through pictures of me and Raejean like I'm a lovesick twelve-year-old. Some of these are from over the summer, from cheer camp. We look tan. We look happy. I remember being happy.

I'm remembering the roundoff–back handspring that I landed wrong, the way my knee puffed up, and how Raejean sat with me the next two nights, changing out my ice pack, blowing off the rest of the girls to read *Cosmo* articles to me. She would find the stupidest sex tips, the ones involving saran wrap or raw steaks, and we would laugh until we were in too much pain to talk.

How could that have been just a few months ago?

Why why why did Coach have to tell me good job today? Why did she have to lay into Raejean?

Raejean has always been the better gymnast, but I'm the

faster learner. She comes out ahead in that equation, because no one keeps track of my learning process, but everyone notices her perfect flips. And that's fine. That's actually great. No spotlight has ever felt as good to me as it feels to be around a happy Raejean. The spotlight makes her happy. That's why she makes a great flyer—and that's why I'm totally happy being too tall to be a flyer. To me, spotlights are pressure; spotlights mean more people watching if you blow it.

The worst part about Raejean avoiding me is that I can't tell if it's real. Maybe she's just distracted. Maybe I'm making this whole thing up. Maybe there is literally nothing wrong whatsoever. And not just with Raejean but with the whole squad. Maybe tomorrow I'll go in, and we'll all be a hive mind again. Maybe no one will make fun of my shoes or some apparently antiquated slang that comes out of my mouth. Maybe this will disappear as quickly as it reared its head.

I'm looking at one of these Instagram photos from the summer, where I have my arms around Raejean from behind and my head on her shoulder. We've been caught mid-laugh. We're both in our sports bras and bike shorts, and you can see muscle definition in our stomachs and arms. I look a little bit like a horse, but happy, and Raejean looks perfect (per usual; she looks like a Disney princess as a general rule).

I don't remember where this was taken.

I comment on the picture: **Where was this? Don't remember this. Amazing pic.**

I hit Enter. I know she has gotten a notification on her phone, I know she is reading my comment right now, but I throw my phone on the bed, bolting out of the room so I can't look at it.

Jack's apparently gone back to his room, which means the living room is empty. Mom's at work, probably until late; she texted earlier. Mom works in public relations, and some of her clients are international, so sometimes she has conference calls at bizarre hours. On those nights she'll come through the door at nine or so, take-out food in one hand—maybe sushi or an avocado wrap—and her last Starbucks of the day in the other, which she sips at the dinner table as Jack and I eat the ginger from her sushi and we all talk about our days. Then Jack and I go to "bed," or at least to our rooms, while Mom camps out on the couch with her laptop, answering the last of her work e-mails.

Maybe tonight I'll pretend I have too much homework to come out of my room. I don't know if I can talk about my day today.

I lie on the blue couch in our living room. The new one that Mom insisted we needed because the old one was faded. It always looked fine to me. There were certain ways you couldn't sit on it without feeling the springs, but I'd mastered the perfect way to lie down for a catnap, and it would be the most comfortable place in the world. I've never been able to sleep on this one. I stare at the ceiling, breathing deeply, trying to run through the routine in my head to drown everything else out.

Up, plié, toe touch, strut strut strut strut, arms to T, arms low V, hands on hips, body roll, back back front, high kick, run run run run,

18

soloists do backflips, back into formation four five six seven prep, tuck jump, spread-eagle, up, plié, toe touch, duck down back line middle front line, pike . . .

Hours later Raejean replies to my Instagram comment with three letters:

idk

Three

I NEED TO BACK UP A SECOND.

The first day of freshman year, Raejean and I were walking around—as we often did—holding hands. We had gotten through five years of friendship holding hands without ever thinking twice about it.

But, freshman year. High school. New games with new rules, which no one bothers to tell you before you enter the ring.

So we were walking down the hallway between first and second period, and these two sophomore guys started following us. We didn't notice until one of them began making kissy noises, the way you might try to summon a cat or a dog. We weren't sure it was aimed at us until one of them yelled out, "Hey, lesbians!"

I wanted to just keep walking and pretend I hadn't heard. But Raejean stopped and turned around, still holding my hand.

They were acne-smeared generic white boys, but they were upperclassmen and we were freshmen and my heart was going at light speed.

But Raejean's lips formed a calm smile as she asked, "What did you say?"

"How's it going, lesbians?" said Generic Sophomore White Dude #2. I don't remember if this really happened, but in my head, a small crowd started gathering.

"We're great," Raejean replied coolly. "How are you?"

They poked each other in the ribs and grinned, big eyed, hands covering their mouths. Raejean rolled her eyes and turned to go, but then one of them yelled out, "Dyke!"

In my mind, the crowd that had gathered by this point all started snickering. I remember some girl yelling, "Oh shit!" but, again, I don't know if that really happened. But here is what I absolutely know to be true: Raejean turned back to the two boys, walked up to the one who had called her a dyke, and punched him in the mouth.

There probably was a commotion. There probably was shouting. What I remember is that the guy had a trickle of blood streaming down the side of his chin. What I remember is the look of pure disoriented shame and awe in his eyes. And I remember that Raejean turned around, grabbed my hand, and walked away.

We never got in trouble. There are some advantages to being female. Raejean calls it the "girl card." Girls can punch boys in the hallway, and no one says shit.

No one ever called us names after that, either, and we kept holding hands in the hallway. She hasn't been holding my hand this school year, though. Not since the Billy incident.

I need to say something else about Raejean.

Ever had a friend that you wanted to crawl inside? Just to hear the noise in their head, feel the movement of their body, the shape of their skin? For as long as I can remember, I have wanted to crawl inside Raejean Winters. And sometimes, I feel like I do.

We went through a summer once when we did trust falls with each other all the time. There'd be no warning. We'd be standing in line for a movie, or at the food court at the mall, and one of us would just cross our arms over our chest and start falling backward. The other person would have to jump into position immediately and prepare to catch the falling girl. We could easily have fallen and cracked our skulls if we hadn't been so inside each other's heads, but we always caught each other.

There was also the time we became blood sisters when we were eleven, feeling our fingers pulse against each other until we weren't sure whose pulse was whose. There were all the times we spotted each other on lifts and jumps, all the times we held each other as we fell asleep and I felt like her heart was beating inside my body.

But the night I felt most like I could crawl inside Raejean was the sophomore-year homecoming dance.

Sophomore year was the year of Mikey Wall. Mikey was six two and biracial with pale green eyes, and he was British—with the accent and everything. Every single girl had a crush on Mikey Wall, but Raejean and I were professionals at it. We would sneak pictures of him on our phones at lunchtime, pretending to take selfies while secretly turning the camera around and zooming in on him. We both kept extensive journals of our every interaction with him, which we would read out loud to each other at night—sometimes on the phone, sometimes in person. We had very, very comprehensive conversations about what oral sex with him would be like.

"I bet Mikey takes his time with a girl," Raejean said. "He must be one of those guys who puts the woman's pleasure first."

"Oh my God," I said, "I think I wrote those words exactly in my diary." I found the passage and showed it to her. One brain, two bodies.

There was no competition. Neither of us had exchanged more than five sentences with him. He was in English class with us, and that was it. But in our fantasy lives, both of us were living a deliciously hedonistic sex life with Mikey Wall. We would write out our fantasies about him in explicit detail—the softness of his lips, nibbles on the earlobe or inner thigh, dirty talk with his hot British accent, the whole thing—and read them out loud to each other. The listener would clutch a pillow, occasionally moaning into it or biting her own fist at a particularly toe-curling passage. We did this for months.

At homecoming that year, Mikey and Raejean started talking at the punch bowl. I remember her laughing radiantly, while I stood by her left elbow, looking down at my drink, wishing I'd picked a different dress. Raejean's dress was crystal white and just low-cut enough to show off her complete lack of tan lines. She looked like a fairy bride. My dress was stone gray, a choice I'd thought was unique and edgy at the time, but the slight shimmer of the fabric was lost in the darkness of the gym, and it was a little too baggy in the waist, and I felt a little bit like I was wearing a trash bag. I wanted to crawl inside her then, to feel what it was like to sparkle like that, with Mikey Wall's warmth enveloping her like a heat lamp.

The DJ changed the track to a slow song, and Mikey asked Raejean, "Would you like to dance?"

She turned to me and giggled, her eyes wide with a kind of *Can you believe this is happening?* But she must have seen something in my face, because her eyes changed and she turned back to Mikey.

"Only if Jenna can come."

He smiled, as only Mikey Wall could smile. "I wouldn't have it any other way."

He took both our hands, and we strode onto the dance floor together. I didn't think it was really happening. I thought there must be some mistake. But we took our place amid all the swaying couples. We each put a hand around his neck, and he put an arm around our waists. "Raejean and Jenna," he said. "Raejenna." And it wasn't as though it was the first time we had heard the joke, but we laughed like it was because his accent made everything funnier.

For the length of a John Legend song, Raejean and I felt

Mikey Wall's hands on our bodies and looked into his round green eyes. We pressed our foreheads against his. The three of us giggled as we swayed back and forth. Over the course of the song, he drew us closer and closer to him, until our thighs brushed against his. We could smell his breath, sweet with a faint trace of whiskey.

From time to time I would look over at Raejean, and we would laugh, smooshing our foreheads and noses together. "Are you two a couple?" Mikey asked.

"No, we're just the same person," Raejean responded.

"Raejenna," we said in unison, and then we all laughed again.

I saw Raejean softly stroking the side of his neck with her fingernails, so I decided to do the same, running my fingertips over his earlobe. We'd smuggled in a flask of Smirnoff under piles of tampons at the bottom of Raejean's bag, and we'd been sneaking sips from it in the bathroom all night. I was feeling bold. He responded by smiling and closing his eyes with a warm "mmmmmmm." I felt his hand tighten on my lower back, slipping down just a couple of inches below where the waistband of my pants would fall. I felt Raejean inhale sharply at the exact moment that I did. His lips were so close to mine, and to hers.

Then the song ended, and the DJ transitioned into Kanye. Mikey pulled away. "Thank you, ladies," he said. He kissed Raejean on the cheek, then me, and he walked away into the crowd.

Raejean's eyes were huge. I was sure mine were, too. We grabbed each other's forearms and screamed, drowned out by the bass of the sound system. I pulled her into my arms, and we squeezed each other so tight it was like we were trying to pop each other. "I'm just trying to absorb as much of his sweat from you as possible," she said, running her hands all over my back. "Oh my God. Did that just happen?"

"I think it did," I said. She pulled back and looked at me.

"You're glowing," she said, and I was sure I was, because she looked like a lightbulb. "Like you're pregnant."

"I think I might've gotten pregnant just now," I replied, laughing.

We danced together for the next five songs, straddling each other's thighs and pressing into each other, far enough into the center of the dance floor that the chaperones around the edge wouldn't see us and tell us to cut it out. We were trying to dance something out that we couldn't release, trying to break through this feeling of restlessness and anticipation in our bellies but just building it up instead. We always moved in perfect rhythm with each other. We could predict each other's moves. We almost merged.

In an alternate version of that night, in a parallel universe that I have imagined a million times, Raejean (Raejean, not me, because she is bolder) whispers in Mikey's ear while we're dancing with him: "You can have both of us, if you want." And Mikey laughs until he sees that she's serious, and that I'm serious, and then he whispers, "Meet me out back," and walks away, and our faces are identical in our utter disbelief, and we gather our purses and our coats and we go out back behind the gym, where his car is idling at the curb. We smoosh into the front seat together, and he drives to a side street and parks the car. Somehow we all get into the back seat, and he kisses one of us, then the other, back and forth, our breath speeding up and filling up the car, fogging up the windows, his hands disappearing up our dresses, while Raejean and I try to keep quiet and fail.

Raejean and I never touch in this scenario. Or maybe we, like, clutch each other's arms, but we don't *do* anything to each other. We come at the exact same time.

Mikey Wall transferred after that semester. I kept following his every move on Facebook until I realized that Raejean no longer jumped in her seat when I showed her a new picture of him, that she had moved on, that now there were soccer players and young substitute teachers on her mind. As soon as I realized that, I stopped thinking about Mikey almost overnight. I couldn't sustain it alone.

I used to tell Raejean point-blank that I wanted to crawl inside her. All the time. She would say it back, or say it first.

I don't think she wants to anymore.

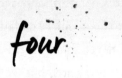

four

IT'S THE NEXT DAY AFTER PRACTICE, AND MEGHAN
Finnegan is putting her hand on my shoulder in the locker room.

"Hey, you all right?"

I look up at her. My eyes fill with tears for a second, and
I quickly blink them away.

"Yeah, why?"

"You just seem a little stressed."

I don't particularly want to vent to Meghan, Meghan who's
been driving Raejean home lately when I've been the one driving
her home since the minute I got my license. Meghan *obviously*
knows that, right? There's no way she could not know that, right?

"I probably am." I shrug and try to laugh.

She sits down on the bench next to me, all confidential. "Just
school and Coach and stuff?"

"Yeah," I say, "yeah, same old."

"Well, if you *want*," she whispers, leaning in closer, "me and Raejean are gonna go smoke a joint in my car. If you wanna join."

I'm sorry, but this is bullshit. *Meghan* is inviting *me* to hang out with her and Raejean? What kind of power-play ridiculousness is this? No, I do not need a friggin' invitation from *you* to see my best friend. Go sit on a public toilet and get herpes.

Also, is this a setup? Isn't this how every single D.A.R.E. PSA starts? I'm probably gonna take a hit from this joint and immediately be swarmed by police and my family and every teacher I've ever had and go to jail for eight billion years. I don't need that shit in my life right now, no, thank you, bye.

Except . . .

I've only tried pot once before, and it didn't really affect me, but who knows? Maybe Meghan's is different. Maybe it would actually relax me. Maybe it would help.

And I miss Raejean.

"Okay. Sure."

"Really?"

"Yeah, just let me finish changing."

"Oh my God, awesome! Okay, see you out there." She bounces out of the locker room.

So this is what Raejean's been doing instead of going home with me. Maybe if I had joints in my purse like Meghan, she'd want to hang out. Maybe I should get on that.

Meghan's car is all the way at the back of the parking lot, a dented blue Chevy Metro from the early 2000s. I suddenly feel better about my four-year-old red Volvo, still pretty much in perfect condition; then my stomach drops again when I realize Raejean must really like Meghan to hang out in this thing.

Raejean and Meghan are already in there. It's a two-door car, so I have to knock on Raejean's window to get in. She looks surprised to see me. Did Meghan not tell her I was coming?

"Oh, hey." She opens the door and scoots her seat forward so I can crawl into the back. They already have the joint lit.

"So he didn't text you?" Meghan asks, passing the joint to Raejean.

"No. I deleted his number so I wouldn't text him first—I don't wanna look desperate." Raejean exhales smoke, stifling a cough. "It's killing me. Like, why did you tell me you like me if you're not gonna text?"

I stick my head forward between their seats. "Who is this?" Am I really asking this? Is there really a guy in Raejean's life who I don't already know about in excruciating detail?

"Marcus Carlsberg," Meghan responds. "My family's foreign exchange student."

"I didn't know you had an exchange student," I say.

"He's a senior, so."

Meghan shows me a picture. Marcus is impossibly gorgeous, with chiseled features and a blue-green stare. My stomach drops. "He's German. From Hamburg," Raejean says. "I call him the Hamburger."

They've got nicknames and everything.

Raejean passes me the joint. "Maybe it's a cultural thing," I offer, trying to meet her eye. "Maybe they don't text the same way in Germany." Raejean keeps looking out the windshield.

"That's racist," Meghan says.

". . . What?"

"Are you racist against Germans, Jenna?"

"No, I'm actually part German . . ."

"I'm totally just messing with you, girl!" She and Raejean crack up. I force a laugh.

I put the joint to my lips and suck in. It's harsher than whatever I smoked the one other time I did pot. That was the last night of cheer camp, when we all sat in a circle on the floor learning how to shotgun. Raejean blew the smoke into my mouth, and I immediately exhaled it; she doubled over laughing: "You're supposed to suck it in! Ditz."

So this time I make sure to suck it in hard, and it scorches my throat and I start coughing, deep chest coughs like when I had bronchitis. I should've refilled my water bottle before I left the locker room, but since I didn't, I just cough and cough. No one offers me a sip of their water.

Meghan is unfazed, taking back the joint and pulling on it flawlessly. "I dunno, Rager," she says, and it takes me a minute before I realize she's talking to Raejean and not talking about a rager of a party. "He keeps asking when you're gonna come over again. He's, like, too much of a gentleman to say flat-out that he wants to hit that? But I think he totally does."

"I dunno," Raejean sighs, leaning her face on her hand and staring out the window. "I just don't get it."

"When *are* you coming over again?" Meghan asks. "My mom's like obsessed with you."

"What about Friday?"

YOU CAN'T GO TO MEGHAN'S ON FRIDAY, RAE-JEAN. YOU HAVE AN EIGHT-PAGE PAPER DUE ON MON-DAY, REMEMBER? AND WHY IS MEGHAN'S MOTHER OBSESSED WITH YOU? THAT'S CREEPY.

The pot is making the top of my head tingle and the edges of my vision kinda fall away, and everything feels like it's happening in slow motion.

"Yeah, that could work." Meghan lets the smoke float out of her mouth, like Frenchy in *Grease*. Raejean watches and giggles.

How are these girls able to carry on conversations like normal people? I feel like I'm made of bricks.

Why didn't Meghan invite me to come over on Friday?

"Jen, you want some more of this?" Meghan's holding the joint out to me.

My name. Is not. Jen.

I'm way too high, but I don't know how to say no, so I take it. I try not to inhale, but I still end up coughing and feeling it harsh in my lungs again. I pass the joint back.

Without my noticing, their conversation has shifted to AP History, which I'm taking, but with Mr. Lee in sixth period, not Mrs. H. in third. I stare out the window. It's raining. The raindrops sound more metallic and all-encompassing than they ever did before.

I realize that I'm gonna have to drive home stoned in the rain.

I feel completely disconnected from reality. I look back at the front seat. Raejean is laughing hard at something, throwing her head back and showing all her teeth. Meghan is . . . freestyling? I guess? About . . . the Civil War?

I lean my forehead against the back of Raejean's seat. I am so, so high. I don't know how to talk or move like a normal person.

It occurs to me that I am going to have to ask one of them to get out of this two-door car to let me out.

Raejean's seat is way too close to my legs. I look at her outstretched legs in the front seat. Why does she need all that leg room? Is she cramping me back here on purpose? To punish me? Show me who's boss?

I try to listen to what they're saying, suddenly terrified that they tried to address a question to me and I missed it. I can't catch the full context—something about period cramps—but it's clear that they are not talking to me.

I look at the clock on Meghan's dashboard. I've somehow only been here for twelve minutes. How is that possible?

It's another thirty before I decide to get out of the car. I don't speak once in those thirty minutes.

They are mid-conversation. Something about vegan recipes. "I'm gonna go home," I announce.

"Oh. Okay," Raejean says. She doesn't look back at me; she doesn't move her seat. I sit there for a moment.

"Can you . . . move your seat up?"

"Oh! Oh right, duh." Who's the ditz now, bitch? She scoots forward but doesn't open the door.

"The door," I say.

"Yeah, yeah," she says, maybe snapping at me a little? I'm too stoned to care. I crawl out. My foot catches on the seat belt a little bit.

Meghan makes a sad *aww* noise as I go. "Bye, girl! Let's do this again!"

I just wave and make my way to my car, raindrops pelting me as I walk. In my driver's seat, I take deep breaths, knowing that I will probably die if I try to drive home.

I have to do something drastic right now, and I don't want to do it, but I really have no choice.

I text Jack:

Are you still at school?

He often stays for several hours after school, playing some vampire version of Dungeons & Dragons with four other seniors who also wear black. My phone and keyboard seem to be in another language, and it takes me about three tries before I overcome the overzealous autocorrect, but I proofread it several times before sending, and it's error-free.

Almost immediately:

Yeah.

I type: **Can you come to the car and drive me home?**

Jack: **Why?**

Me: **Please?**

34

When he gets in the car, he clocks what's going on immediately and can't stop laughing. I personally don't find it funny. "Oh man, do you owe me," he keeps saying. "You owe me so hard for this one."

"Don't tell Mom," I say.

"I know, Jenna. I'm not a snitch. But you so owe me."

The motion of the car makes me queasy. I roll down the window. "You're gonna get the passenger side wet," he says.

"I don't care."

I let the rain and the cold wind hit me in the face, and I feel a little bit less like I'm going to throw up.

"Wow," he says. "You are so stoned."

"Yeah."

I feel like crying, but my machinery is so slowed down and disconnected that I literally don't know how.

five

HEATHER IS REVIEWING OUR HOMECOMING
routine with us.

I know I haven't mentioned Heather yet. Heather is many
things, among them: a first-generation Polish American, a senior, a beacon of fierce stage presence when she's cheering and
often barely audible when she speaks, pale as milk, bad at small
talk, a magnificent choreographer. We're not particularly close.

Competition season doesn't really start until next month in
November, and Coach Mason (her real name's Louise, but no
one calls her that) always choreographs those routines, but
homecoming is *ours*; it's always choreographed by a student. In
competition dances, there are certain moves you just have to do
if you want to even be considered—certain spins, flips, stunts,
whatever. Judges frown on too much cross-pollination of dance
genres or anything too sexual.

But at homecoming we can do whatever we want.

Heather is standing in front of us demonstrating the moves. Rather than "and five and six and seven and eight," she'll clap the numbers. "And [*clap*] and [*clap*] and [*clap*] and [*clap*]." I think it's because talking in front of people makes her nervous. And when she has to explain the move to us in her slight Polish accent, we all have to lean forward to hear her, to understand, holding our breaths so we don't miss a word. I used to be frustrated by her soft voice, but I'm no longer bothered by it; I find it hypnotic, even soothing. "So we begin in a handstand . . ."

As awkward, as whispery, as weird as Heather is, her choreography is the exact opposite. When you do Heather's choreography, you feel like a pop star. It's got hip-hop and jazz and some things I don't even know the name of and a million lifts. It's guaranteed to be a crowd-pleaser. Even for people who think cheerleading is stupid.

(I've heard Heather talking to her mom in Polish. She's much louder when she speaks Polish.)

We all knew she'd be choreographing homecoming. A lot of us thought she should've choreographed last year's homecoming, too, but Anna Marquez had gotten it because she was a senior. Anna's style was more ass shaking, less skill. But now that Heather's a senior, there was no reason for her not to get it this year. Even the girls who find Heather annoying, who privately imitate her quiet accent and her doe-eyed gaze, can't deny her brilliance. Even those girls—snooty sophomore Evelyn Rice and her doppelgänger, Melissa Markham, mostly—will suck it up and lean in to hear Heather's soft voice for the sake of her chore-ography.

We start on our hands—me, Jodi Lin, Ebony Starker, and Raejean. You do a handstand, but instead of your legs straight up in the air, you bend them at opposite angles like you're riding a bike. You switch your legs back and forth really fast, and then on the seventh beat you hold for eight. Switch switch switch switch switch switch switch HOLD, switch switch switch switch switch switch switch HOLD . . .

Then we dismount, and Meghan and Becca and Mandy Lockley all do the worm across the stage while the rest of us do this casual skip-saunter thing into formation . . .

Then it gets fast: arms high V, then daggers, then hands to your forehead while you pop your ass back, right leg over left, turn around 360 degrees and smack your hips, snake your head right, straight, right elbow and left knee to the chest, step down, arms in a pike and hips go right, left, right, clasp, half the girls do center splits down to the floor, roll onto your tummy and bring your legs together behind you, roll to the right, onto your back, and then the other half of the girls do a front walkover above you as you bring your legs up in the air and spot her with your hands—

And then your partner is lying flat on your feet, suspended in the air, while you lie on the ground beneath her, your legs holding her up, looking up at her back. She floats.

I love this move. It feels like magic every time it happens, whether I'm the flyer or the base.

But today I'm worried that I will drop my partner, Evelyn Rice with the resting bitch face.

It's one of the easier lifts; Coach told us that women naturally have more lower-body strength than upper, so any lift where you can use your legs instead of your arms is a dream.

Still.

We practice the lift without incident, and without smiling. Heather watches us and smiles for us. "Good job."

Then there are the one-armed push-ups. ONE-ARMED PUSH-UPS. Everyone bitched and moaned when she introduced that part of the number. But when there's an army of teenage girls doing one-armed push-ups in unison, you kind of just have to stand in awe.

There are also four basket tosses in unison. Four groups, four flyers—Raejean, Evelyn, Jodi, and Becca—all soaring into the air at once with a toe-touch jump before descending safely to the arms of their bases.

I love this routine.

I am trying to focus on how much I love this routine.

We've been learning this routine for the past week, but today for some reason I can't stop staring at Heather, wondering what it's like to walk around in her paper-white skin, to talk through her whispering mouth. Is she okay? Is she happy? Have I ever seen her have fun offstage?

Everyone respects Heather, but I don't think anyone *likes* Heather. Not actively. Like, people are *fine* with Heather. She wears the same gray baggy sweatshirt every day, with her fine dark bangs sticking to her forehead, and she'll smile at you when you say hi, and that's the end of it.

Is this what my future looks like?

Am I going to be a Heather?

Is this squad going to inside-joke me into a pale, whispering loner?

With Heather, I can at least justify it because she's a genius. Geniuses are loners all the time. Geniuses find their people later in life, and it's fine.

I am not a genius.

I'm just a fast learner who can do the splits.

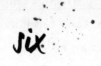

six

OUR FOOTBALL TEAM IS A JOKE, BY THE WAY. THE
Marsen High School Puffins. No, I'm not kidding. The Puffins.
The friggin' *Puffins*. I cheer for a football team that calls them-
selves the *Puffins*. Let that sink in.

It wouldn't be so funny if they won more often. On the rare
occasion that they do win, Meghan will often shout, "You just
got demolished by the Puffins!" Alas, our football players are
only slightly more intimidating than a bowl of cereal.

I would say that at least half our crowds come to see the
cheer squad, not the football team. Even Jack has come tonight
to the homecoming game, mostly because Mom dragged him
here.

I look into the stands and see Mom bedecked in purple and
yellow, a sharp contrast to Jack's black couture. She screams and
screams: "Go, Puffins!"

Hovering at the sidelines with our pom-poms vibrating, we yell across the field at the Centurions' cheerleaders.

"Be! Afraid! Be, be, afraid! Be! Afraid! Be, be, afraid!

"Centurions, be alarmed! Centurions will be! Dis! Armed!

"P-U-F-F-I-N-S, can't touch us 'cause we're the best! P-U-F-F-I-N-S, pride and joy of MHS!

"Centurions are goin' down! You know Puffins run this town!

"Be! Afraid! Be, be, afraid!

"Centurions! Run and hide! Feel that purple-yellow pride!"

Raejean wields her pom-poms like weapons. I wield my pom-poms like I'm holding a wet dog.

Heather belts it out confidently on the cheers. I wonder if she had to train herself to project her voice. I look over at her, and she's all sassy hips and beaming smiles. I try to channel her.

We're only a quarter in, but the Puffins are losing. They're probably gonna keep losing. Gary Takahashi screws up a tackle, but then he takes off his helmet and shakes out his shiny black hair, and all the girls in the bleachers scream.

At halftime we finally get to do Heather's routine, the only thing I like about being here anymore. The music feels like it's lighting a fire inside me: *Boom boom boom boom boom boom kick it . . .*

When we perform, we are one. We are an octopus, all just limbs of a greater whole. Our timing and our balance and our smiles are all so effortlessly perfect, and I can feel the crowd just losing. Their. *Minds.*

This is my drug. Screw alcohol; screw pot. Regular substances can't hold a candle to the sound of a crowd roaring after four simultaneous basket tosses. The exhilaration of getting the jump exactly right, of when the timing works out flawlessly and we're all in a triangle formation kicking our legs to the exact same height.

Alas, my drug of choice only ever lasts for three minutes at a time.

The routine ends. The crowd goes ballistic. And then we have to go back to the sidelines, back to yelling chants at the Centurion cheerleaders, back to feeling totally alone in my own body.

The Puffins, improbably, win the game.

seven

AT THE PARTY AFTER THE GAME, I DRINK AS quickly as possible. I scoop bright pink-purple punch into my clear plastic cup, and then I grab the vodka and spike my already-spiked concoction.

We're at Becca Ruiz's enormous house, with a backyard that goes on for days and a kitchen with white marble counters. I don't know what her parents do, or why they're not here, and I don't care.

Everyone but me is high from the game, high from the win, but no one is talking to me unless I talk to them first, and I'm tired of initiating. So I wander.

I learned the party-wandering trick as a freshman on JV. If you're a loner at a party, but you just keep moving, no one will notice. They're too engrossed in their own conversations and choreography and tonsil hockey. You move until someone gives you a reason to stop.

I wander my way through my first glass of punch, watching as my teammates grind on the living room dance floor, watching jocks sneak their arms around bare shoulders like they think the girl won't notice, watching a beer fall sideways onto the hardwood floor and Becca yelling in Spanish; then I go back and refill.

I don't know where Raejean is, and this bothers me more than it should. I'm sick of hearing myself think about it.

I resume wandering, second extra-vodka punch in hand, and this time I wander outside. Lots of lit cigarettes, girls dangling their pedicures in Becca's pool, and Meghan and Raejean huddled together in a corner of the lawn, thumb wrestling.

I watch for a while, trying to catch either of their eyes, but they're focused. Meghan keeps winning.

"Hey," I finally say.

"Jennaaaaaaaa!" Meghan squeals.

I'm pissed off by her niceness, but I saunter over to them all casual, like this is just one of many social stops I have to make tonight, like we're just gonna have a chill three-minute conversation like friendly acquaintances and then move on with our lives.

"What's up?" I say, like a douche.

"Meghan was just kicking my ass at thumb wrestling," Raejean giggles, addressing it to me but still looking at Meghan.

"Well that's not fair," I say. "Meghan's hands are bigger. Of course she won."

"Are you making fun of my hands, Jenna?" Meghan stares at me incredulously.

I think she's doing her thing, that thing where she makes you feel like you've said something awful and then laughs at you for believing her, so I just stare at her. Sure enough, she busts up laughing and points in my face. "Just kidding!"

"It's not a good joke if you have to explain that it's a joke," I say.

Meghan stops laughing and just looks at me. Raejean is looking at me, too. Like I farted or something.

I don't care. I hold out my hand. "Can I play winner?"

"My hands are sore from beating RJ here," Meghan says, and what IS it with these two and their effing nicknames?!

"Or you're just worried you'll lose," I say, trying to laugh as I say it.

Meghan laughs a little, too, but suddenly we're fifth-grade boys or something, and now this is a real competition with real stakes. It's thumb wrestling, for Pete's sake, but as she smiles, her eyes get harder.

"Hell no. I'd beat you with my big man hands."

I shrug. "Best two out of three?"

"What does the winner get?" she responds.

I think for a second, and I don't know why, but this is what comes out of my mouth:

"Nothing. *Loser* gets a slap in the face from Raejean."

Raejean looks a little bit like she did the afternoon I poured water on her head, but Meghan is laughing and clapping her hands together. "Yo, that's *sick*, dude!"

Raejean laughs nervously, "Don't drag me into this," but she can see that Meghan loves the idea, and *that* is what's convincing her to go along with it.

"All right, let's do this. Let's go." Meghan adjusts her sleeves, crouches down, holds out her arm. I hold out mine. We lock eyes.

"Guys, I don't wanna slap you," Raejean whimpers from the side, but we act like we don't hear her.

"One two three four I declare a thumb war!"

Meghan's victory is almost instantaneous, her long thumb clamping down on mine and staying put for the required ten seconds. We shake it out; we exhale; we lock eyes; we join hands.

"One two three four I declare a thumb war!"

This time it's more of a wrestle, more of a back-and-forth. Her long thumb hovers perpendicular, like a skyscraper, occasionally swooping down to try to take down mine, but I keep mine stretched as far back as I can. After she's done this three or four times, I catch her off guard, pinning her down. "One two three four five six—" And then she wiggles out, but I dive-bomb again almost immediately, and this time I press down hard, really hard; I don't care if I break her thumb. "One two three four five six seven eight nine TEN!" And I win.

We break. We shake it off. "Best outta three, best outta three," Meghan mutters to herself.

"I really don't wanna slap either of you," Raejean says again, but Meghan is so focused I'm not even sure she hears Raejean. Eye contact, hands, go.

"One two three four I declare a thumb war!"

Another standoff. Thumbs straight up. She makes a couple of swipes for mine, but I hold back. I realize I could beat her again. And then I realize, almost in the same breath, that what I really want is to lose.

I make a swipe for her thumb, I'm clumsy on purpose, and she slams my thumb into my hand. "One two three four five six seven eight . . . nine . . . TEN! Boom!" She even stretches the last three numbers out, like pointing out how long she was pinning me, like I hadn't let her win.

Raejean is making a pouty face, and I kind of hate her right now. "I don't wanna hit you," she says.

"But Meghan won," I respond, almost scaring myself with how calm I am.

I can tell that Meghan wants Raejean to slap me but doesn't feel like she can say so. "You don't have to do it, like, *hard*," she says.

"No, do it hard," I say. "Really hit me."

"You are like . . . *sick*," Raejean says, smiling, trying to make it a joke.

"Just do it," I say. "Just do it, and get it over with."

She gives me a teeny girly excuse for a slap. "There," she says.

"No, come on," I say. "You can do better than that."

She does it again, a little harder. "That's not a real slap," I say.

A couple of guys nearby have started watching us (because if there's one thing guys love to see more than girls kissing, it's girls fighting). I smile as I realize two things simultaneously: One, Raejean can't back out now; two, I am dah-*runk*.

She slaps me, and this time it actually stings. "Do it again," I say.

"What is *up* with you?" she hisses.

"Do it again!" I say, smiling bigger. "It's fun! Do it again!"

Boys are softly chanting: "Fight, fight, fight, fight." "Hit her again!" "Do it!" She hits me once, twice, three times, each time harder than the last. An all-consuming belly laugh overtakes me, and I bend over a little, I'm laughing so hard. I don't know why I'm laughing, but I ask her to slap me again.

This time she hits me so hard I actually lose a little bit of my vision for a moment. When my sight comes back to full, I look at her and see that her eyes are red. She's scowling in a way I've only seen her do when she fights with her mom.

"Why are you so *weird* lately?"

And she stomps off into the house.

Boys are shouting at me: "Yo, what'd you do to her?" "That was nuts!" "Hooooo shit, son!" But I feel very quiet, very still, watching her walk away. I half expect Meghan to follow her, but she's addressing our audience, trying to disperse them. "All right, show's over, boys. Come on."

One of them pokes me in the ribs as he walks away: "Yo, I dunno what you did to piss that girl off, but that shit was *awesome*."

49

Meghan pulls a cigarette out of a box I didn't even realize she was holding. "You want one?" she asks me.

I don't answer. I walk inside, pick up my purse, and walk out the front door.

Okay then, I keep saying in my head. *Okay then. Okay then. Okay then. Okay then. Okay then.*

I guess I've lost her.

Okay then.

eight

I WALK TO THE CORNER AND SUMMON A CAR WITH
my phone; Mom made me install the app when I got my driver's
license, "just so, in case anything happens, you always have a way
to get home." I wonder if she knew at the time that I'd use it to
keep from driving drunk.

I'll have to pick up my car from Becca's tomorrow, but I'll
deal with that later. Right now I just need to get home without
seeing anyone else on my way out. Fortunately, no one ventures
far enough from the front yard to see me, and I get home without incident.

The first thing to do is burn Raejean's letters. I have binders
full of them, stretching all the way back to fourth grade, actual
paper-and-pencil physical letters; we used to exchange them
daily before switching to phones, and sometimes even after.
When the car drops me off, I slam through the front door, grab

a cookie sheet from the kitchen counter, ignore Jack when he asks what I'm doing, and hide in my room. Door locked, lighter out, let's do this. I don't even bother to take off my stilettos.

I open up my "memory box," the cardboard box in my closet of stuff from when I was a kid, and start to drag out binders of letters. There're notes from other kids, too, but mostly Raejean. I light the corner of the very first letter.

I feel sick. I drank too fast. I chug my water bottle as the paper burns.

There's a knock. Shit. I put out the fire with the water and yell at my bedroom door. "WHAT?"

The door rattles. Another knock. I hear Jack's voice: "Can you unlock it?"

I sigh and open the door. "Can I help you?"

He points at the cookie sheet. "I need that."

"Why do you need that." I'm too tired for question marks, too tired to change my inflection at the end of the sentence.

"Why do YOU need that?"

"I asked you first."

"Because I'm making cookies? That's why I had it out?"

"Fine. FINE." I remove the soggy half-burned letter and shove the tray at him. He takes it but doesn't move. He's just looking at me. "WHAT."

"Are you burning stuff?"

"No." I know from his face he doesn't buy the lie.

"Jenna, I don't know if you know this, but burning shit while you're drunk is a REALLY BAD IDEA."

It somehow hadn't occurred to me that Jack might be able to tell that I was drunk.

"I have water," I say, looking at the floor.

"I don't care! Don't set things on fire when you're drunk! That's just not smart!" I don't say anything, don't look up. We stand there for a while. He looks past me into my bedroom and sees the binders of childhood letters. "You okay?" he finally asks.

Blink blink. Was that English? Am I okay? What does the word *okay* even mean? Why is someone who thinks everything I do is stupid asking me this question? I stare back at him and finally say, "Since when do you care if I'm okay?"

He exhales hard and squints his eyes shut like he's been stung. Very quietly, he says, "That was a shitty thing to say."

Oh Jesus. I can see the trademark family blush of shame rushing over his face. Can't I get through this night without destroying any more of my relationships?

"Sorry," I mutter. "I'm just drunk. I didn't mean that."

He shrugs, even though I can tell he's still hurt. "Cookies'll be ready in like twenty minutes. If you want any."

". . . Nnnnnno. Shouldn't. Sugar."

"Why do you even diet? You're already skinny. It's like you hate joy."

"BECAUSE I'M AN ATHLETE, YOU IDIOT."

"'Kay. Well. You should probably eat something. So you don't get a hangover."

Shit. If Jack knows I'm drunk, Mom will *definitely* know. "Is Mom up?"

"No, Mom's not up."

"'Kay. Good."

"The cookie offer stands if you change your mind."

I close the door without responding. Then I open it again immediately. "Who makes cookies at *midnight?*"

He laughs. I'm not kidding. Who *does* that?

I close the door again, I look around, I dig a Luna bar out of a desk drawer and bite off a small corner. It tastes like sawdust.

I return to the binder and start to methodically rip up letters.

nine

AT SIX A.M., THE ALARM I SET GOES OFF, AND I TAKE
another car to Becca's to pick mine up; it's still there on the
street where I left it. Back home, I creep through the front door
cautiously, but Mom's still not up. Good.

I zonk out for a few more hours, and when I wake up at ten,
my phone has a cheerful reminder on the screen: **Homecoming
dance tonight!**

Shit. That's right. It's Saturday.

Mom took me shopping for my dress a few weeks ago, when
things had just started getting weird with Raejean. Not that
I couldn't have gone alone, but Mom suggested it. "We can get
our nails done afterward!"

Back when Dad was still at home, he used to tease her about
anything she did that was remotely quote-unquote feminine.
"Your goopy, girly shit," he'd say about her various bath and hair

products. "Your frilly, froofy shit" referred to her slips and bras. She would giggle, but her laughter always sounded dutiful and automatic.

When he left, I think she was excited to indulge her unabashedly femme side and was always disappointed any time I didn't want to play along. I was ten, when kids suddenly start worrying about being "cool," and I didn't want my mom to do my makeup for dance recitals, I didn't want her to pick my dresses, I didn't want her to style my hair, and more than once I saw her blink back tears when I brushed her off.

I still don't entrust her with any aspect of my appearance. But she gets excited about dresses, and I get excited about free manicures. So, fine. We went to the Mission Valley mall.

Not wanting to repeat last year's gray-garbage-bag mistake, I opted for the girliest dress I could find: pale pink, strappy, with a rhinestone appliqué in the center of the chest and layers of shimmery chiffon. I felt a little bit like a wedding cake or a doily, but I convinced myself, looking in the mirror, that it would look right with my hair and makeup done. Mom nearly swooned when I came out of the dressing room in it. "You look like a movie star," she gushed, hands over her heart.

But tonight, still hungover from Becca's party, I feel like overkill personified. This dress is trying way too hard. This dress is desperate. I look like a five-year-old playing princess.

I consider changing my outfit. I consider not going. But everything else in my closet is too casual, and I don't want to deal with explaining to Mom why I'm staying home, or lying to her and finding somewhere else to go for four hours.

Most dances, Raejean and I get ready together. She comes over with a box of makeup and a gallon of hair spray, and we blast Beyoncé and hover over my mirror, and my mom gushes over us and takes pictures. Today I wondered all day if Raejean might text me to say she's not coming, but radio silence. I apply my lip gloss alone. I can't even stand to listen to music; I associate it all with her.

My mom still gushes. She still takes pictures. Jack glides through the living room while she does this, munching on one of his midnight cookies. "Jack, doesn't your sister look nice?"

"You look like Princess Peach," he says. I don't know what that means. He disappears.

"Where's Raejean?" Mom asks. She's got her glasses perched halfway down her nose, looking over the rims at the smartphone she doesn't understand, trying to figure out how to zoom in on me.

"She's heading there with Meghan, I think."

"Meghan could come over, too, if she wanted."

"I don't know. Um. Meghan's got a foreign exchange student that Raejean has a crush on, so . . ." Mom makes a fake scandalized face. I know I'm telling the truth, but the million omissions make it feel like a lie.

"Why didn't you go to Meghan's?"

"Oh, her place isn't that big. It just made more sense to meet them there." Please, Mom, I'm begging you, stop talking about Raejean.

"Do you know how to make the screen go closer?" Thank God.

My mom goes to Zumba classes and doesn't eat gluten, but she's fifty and she can't keep all the softness out of her figure. She claims not to mind. "At my age, I've *earned* these extra pounds," she laughs sometimes, but then she also weighs herself obsessively.

We look enough alike that people ask if we're sisters. As I poke at her phone's screen, I can't help but think that when she sees me all dressed up, or in my cheer uniform, she feels like she can be skinny again for a second. I feel evil as soon as I've had the thought.

I also consider pretending I don't know how to make her phone camera zoom in, because I want as little documentation of this moment as possible, but it only takes a moment to show her, less time than it would take me to think of how to lie.

"You'll be home by midnight?" Mom asks as I get my jacket.

I roll my eyes. There is no way I'm lasting until midnight. "Yeah, Mom."

"And tomorrow you need to do those dishes in the sink."

"Yeah, I know."

Mom drops her stern look, letting her face flood with a beaming smile. "You look so pretty, honey." I just hang my head awkwardly.

My mom's name is Sue. Sue Watson. Raejean calls her Swatson:

"Lookin' good, Mama Swatson!" Actually, most of the time, Raejean calls my mom "Mom." I mean, she used to. They had their own inside jokes that I wasn't even always allowed in on, but I loved that; it somehow made me feel even closer to Raejean.

What am I gonna do when I see her tonight?

Mom gives me a big gushy kiss on the cheek as I head out the door. "Be safe!"

Don't worry, Mom. Last year we snuck in a flask, but this year I'm going straight-edge. Substances have not been kind to me lately.

My hands shake on the car ride. I'm half expecting some *Carrie* shit to go down tonight. It's not too late to ditch the dance, I guess, but I've already done my hair and I'm already on my way and then I'm already there, presenting my ticket and getting my wristband and getting my purse searched and shuffling into the gym.

I can see most of the squad in their (our?) usual corner of the gym, clustered around one of the big round tables, like it's a wedding reception. Raejean's dress is short and bloodred and one-shouldered and backless, all sharp angles and tight satin. Meghan's got almost the same dress on, but it's emerald green and the neckline's different. In fact, just about everyone seems to have gone for short dresses, in bright jewel tones like turquoise and purple and sapphire and orange, and like 80 percent of them have the same strappy black heels. They look incredible, like some kind of superhero squad.

Why didn't anyone tell me this was short-dress year? Why didn't anyone tell me not to wear pastels?

I start to sit down in a chair that looks empty, but then Evelyn Rice pokes her smug little face at me. "Sorryyyyy, that's *my* chair," she says with a fake smile, holding her arm out to stop me from sitting.

"You are a sophomore. It's my chair," I reply, and I sit my ass down. I can feel her making a stank face at me, but I don't look.

Only a couple of people notice this exchange; it's kind of like it isn't happening, like I haven't actually arrived and I'm not actually sitting at this table and taking up space. Raejean is steadfastly avoiding eye contact with me, or maybe she genuinely hasn't seen me come in. Maybe I look so much like a knockoff Disney princess that she doesn't recognize me.

You've lost her, remember?

Becca Ruiz pulls her chair close to mine. "Hey, girl, where'd you go last night? You totally ghosted on us," she says. "You get your car back okay?"

I start to fumble my way through an excuse, something about not feeling well, but then Jodi Lin giggles her way over to Becca and whispers something in her ear; Becca starts giggling, too. "Oh my God, are you serious?" And the two of them pull away from the group, whispering and squealing, without so much as an "Excuse me" from Becca.

I think I was eight when I realized you could be surrounded by people and still be alone. At the time it was more of a philosophical musing, wonderment at the imprecision of words; I didn't feel particularly alone when I realized it. It wasn't a sad thing for me.

That was half my lifetime ago.

Raejean and I accidentally make eye contact across the table. I can't not smile at her, though I'm sure it must look small and forced; she smiles back, and it looks just as small and forced. "You look nice," I say.

"What?" she half shouts.

"You look nice!"

"I can't hear you!"

"I said you look nice!" She just nods and smiles; she didn't actually hear me. I want her to tell me I look nice, too, but she won't. She pretends to get distracted by something across the room.

Actually, maybe she's not pretending, because I follow her gaze and see Heather. Heather seems to be the one other person at this dance wearing a long, flowy dress, lavender and sparkly with a matching shawl. She's with some super-tall goateed guy I don't recognize. Heather looks pretty, but out of place. Like she should be a bridesmaid or something. But she looks . . . *happy*. She's holding hands with her gigantic date and just beaming, glowing like I've only seen her glow when she performs. I didn't know she had a boyfriend.

They pass our table, and everyone says hi to Heather, and she does kind of a princess wave, but she doesn't stop. They're sitting at their own table, I guess. They're in their own little world.

No one's dancing yet. If there was dancing, I could press my way to the middle of the dance floor and be invisible.

I decide to start walking in circles.

I'll start with the bathroom, take a really long time, reapply lipstick, and maybe when I come back, there'll be more people dancing and I can hide on the dance floor.

As I make my way to the back of the gym, I pass Jack and his friends: lanky, white Karissa with the round Harry Potter–style glasses, whose long, frizzy hair falls down her back beneath her top hat; Axel, her boyfriend, who is short and round and black and mid-laughter; Andraleia, looking like a tiny Morticia Addams, dancing by herself; and Gemma, with her tuxedo and slicked-back short light-brown hair, staring into space with her hands in her pockets, bouncing gently to the music. Jack and Gemma were buddies as kids, and then the others came along in seventh grade. Since middle school, the five of them have been an inseparable blob, sometimes invading our kitchen and mixing pink lemonade powder with grape soda, tossing out *Hey, Jenna*s as I make my way past them. They're nice enough, but mostly we just stay out of one another's way.

Gemma's eyes briefly flicker to mine, and she gives a half-hearted wave; I squeak out a smile. Jack also sees me, but we mutually agree with our eyes to pretend it didn't happen.

Bathroom. A few freshman girls exclaiming too loudly, their voices too high, just *sooo* excited for tonight and *ohhhh* my Gaaawwwwd I just *looove* your *dresssss* . . . I shut myself into a stall and breathe until they leave. Was I ever that loud and over-the-top? I don't think I was.

When I confront the mirror, I'm immediately annoyed with myself. Who is that overdressed girl in the princess gown? Why is she trying so hard? My makeup is too much. I wipe half of it off.

I haven't even been here half an hour.

The theme tonight is "A Night to Remember." What does that even mean? Who came up with this shit? Whatever it means, every spare surface in the gym has been covered with glitter. Gold glitter paint squiggles on the mirror in the bathroom. Pink glitter streamer curtains in the doorways. I've never been to Las Vegas, but this is how I imagine it, garish and sparkly and oppressive. My teammates, in their sleek jewel-tone uniforms, make the decorations look even tackier by comparison. My fluffy sparklebomb of a dress blends in with the decor.

I'm getting too depressed looking at myself. I need to get out of here. Maybe someone's started dancing by now.

When I emerge from the bathroom, there's like ten people on the dance floor. No one I know; maybe they're freshmen. I hover at the back of the gym and look over to the cheerleader table. A tall blond guy is sitting between Meghan and Raejean. I recognize him, but I don't know why. Then Meghan's head falls backward with laughter, and it all clicks: *Marcus Carlsberg, German Foreign Exchange Student*. He is every bit as stunning as his photo—more so, even. He's wearing a sleek cobalt-blue suit, which looks like it's tailored, and his golden-blond hair is slicked back in this perfect little puff that somehow doesn't look douchey. Raejean is leaning toward him, talking animatedly, her hand on his knee. Raejean has always been a better flirt than me. I can only flirt with guys I find mildly attractive; too hot and I forget basic English.

He's cute. Good for her. Raejean deserves a cute guy.

The DJ puts on a slow jam, one of those songs I know all the words to, but I have no clue who sings it or what it's called, one of those Top 40 mall jams. I wonder if Billy Nguyen is here? It suddenly occurs to me that amid all the squad shenanigans since his birthday party, I haven't really thought about him. Maybe he's here. Maybe he's forgotten about the glass of water. Maybe he wants to slow-dance. I start wandering the perimeter of the room, looking around.

Marcus and Raejean and Meghan get up from the table together and head to the dance floor. I watch them passively for a moment before I realize what's going on. Meghan and Raejean are each holding one of Marcus's hands and staring at each other with wide-eyed grins, their faces pure, open-mouthed *Can you believe this is happening?!* And all at once my stomach turns into a boulder.

Mikey Wall.

They're gonna Mikey Wall this guy.

That was our thing. *That was our thing.* Raejean and Meghan have probably been exchanging filthy diary entries about Marcus Carlsberg (which is not nearly as hot a name as Mikey Wall, sorry), fantasizing out loud in each other's bedrooms, writing their little German-Ken-doll fan fiction. Maybe it's not even fantasizing. Maybe one or both of them have already hooked up with him. Maybe they're in a three-way relationship. Maybe they've been having threesomes on the weekend in the back of Meghan's shitty Chevy Metro.

Raejean sees me, and her face does this weird wiggle for a

minute. There's no way she doesn't know what I'm thinking. But it only lasts a second, and then she looks back at Marcus and smiles. She and Meghan each hook an arm around his neck, and he slips his hands into the small of Raejean's back, the curve of Meghan's waist. They dance close.

I need some air.

I slip out through the back door, and instead of heading left into the parking lot, I turn right toward the academic buildings and start wandering without a plan. It's cool tonight, a nice respite from the sweaty air of the gym. My heels make a conspicuous little *clack, clack, clack* on the concrete. I walk past the art building, past the drama classroom and auditorium; I walk until I'm a sufficient distance from the gym, and then I scream at the top of my lungs.

It feels good. All the echoing. All the metal and concrete bouncing my scream back at me. All the empty space around me just holding the sound, suspended. It's gratifying. I laugh a little. I scream again, and again hear the buzzing of my echo.

Then I hear the little *clack, clack, clack* of high heels on concrete and low murmuring voices.

Shit. Shit shit shit. I try to tiptoe away from the sound of the heels, around the corner, but I'm not fast enough.

"Jenna?"

I turn around. It's Heather, with her eight-foot-tall boyfriend. She looks flustered and giggly and concerned all at once. "Are you all right?"

I'm about to answer her but stop when I look from her to

her date and back again. His mouth is a little red, and their hair is messy. *Why were they out here?* I think, and then: *Oh.* They were making out. Of course. Why didn't it occur to me that Heather might sneak off to make out with someone? Why is literally everyone having a better night than me tonight?

"Yeah," I say. "Yeah, I'm fine."

"Was that you screaming?" Her voice is so . . . clear? So confident and resonant, not whispery or understated at all. I've never heard it like this before when she wasn't cheering.

"Yeah, yeah, I, uh . . . I saw a shadow, and I thought it was, um . . . I dunno what I thought it was. Everything's okay, though."

She smiles. She's so radiant. "Are you having a good night?"

I don't want to ruin her night by being honest. "Yeah," I say. "I just needed some fresh air. What about you?"

She giggles and squeezes her guy's hand. "Great night," she says. "This is Adam."

"Hi," I say. "Jenna."

Adam shakes my hand. His hand is the size of my head.

"How'd, uh, how'd you two meet?" I ask.

"Church," Adam says. His voice is so low, like it's coming out of the ground.

"Cool. Well. I guess I better head back."

"Bye, Jenna!" Heather calls after me as I clack my way to the gym.

When I get inside again, people are dancing, including pretty much everyone from the cheer table. Good. I won't have to figure out what to say to them. I thought I wanted to dance, but it sounds kind of terrible right now. Standing around with a bunch of strangers, moving my body for no reason, hiding from my friends-turned-distant-acquaintances.

I slump in my chair, checking my phone, as if anyone was going to text me, trying to convey with my posture that I am above it all, that I give no shits, that dancing is for losers who don't care if they look like oversexed jellyfish on the dance floor. I play Candy Crush until I run out of lives, and then I decide to hit the bathroom again. It's empty this time, thank God. My lipstick looks fine, but I reapply it anyway. Something to do.

Briefly, I consider dousing my face and hair and entire body in water and returning to the dance floor soaking wet, makeup sliding down my cheeks, princess gown slicked to my skin and leaving puddles in its wake.

The urge passes.

Maybe I should just go home.

I come out and see Jack's friend Gemma again, elegant in her tuxedo, staring intently at the bathroom door. I startle her. "Oh. Hey," she sputters, looking at the floor.

"Hey, there's no one in there, if you were waiting or something . . ."

"Oh. Ummmm." Her eyes jump all over the place. "Okay. Um. Would you do me a favor?"

"Sure?"

"Can you just . . . stand out here and make sure no one comes in? I'll just be a second."

"Okay. Uh. Yeah, sure." I don't ask why. Maybe Gemma's having a rough night, too. Gemma and Jenna. Ha.

"Thank you *so* much. I'll be super fast." She rushes in. I wonder if she's doing coke in there or something. Malia, a senior girl, got kicked off the team last year for doing coke; I hadn't realized at the time that she was doing it, but I had noticed that she was always darting into bathrooms abruptly.

No one comes by, and soon Gemma pops out again. "Thanks so much, man, really appreciate it."

"Yeah, no problem."

"You gonna go dance?"

"Oh, uh . . . I dunno. I might go home soon, actually."

"Really?!"

"Yeah, I dunno."

"It's not even nine o'clock!"

"Yeah, I dunno. I just . . . I'm not having a great time."

"Oh. I'm sorry to hear that."

"Yeah, no, it's fine. I just might call it a night."

"But you look so nice."

I laugh, looking at her black tux, thinking about Jack and all their black-clad friends. I look down at my pink sparklebomb failure of a dress. "You don't have to say that," I say.

"No, I mean it. You do."

"I've decided I don't really like this dress."

"No, it's pretty. You've got like a Galadriel thing going on."

I don't know what that means, and I don't ask. "Thank you," I say, still not really believing her. "You look nice, too."

Gemma shrugs off the compliment, and I don't have the energy to convince her that I mean it. "If you dance to just one song and *then* go, at least you'll know you gave it a shot," she says. "Or maybe you'll dance to one song and then decide to stay. But at least you'll know."

Why are you so invested in me dancing? I wanna ask. But I just shrug. Maybe it's the coke? "All right."

"You gonna dance?"

"Yeah. I guess."

"Cool. Me too."

We walk back to the dance floor. I can see the whole cheer team in their own little circle, grinding on each other and giggling. I stand about twenty feet away. No one I know is around me, except Gemma and some girl from sophomore-year English. We dance to Rihanna.

Gemma is an incredibly enthusiastic dancer, pumping her fists in the air, crouching low and then popping up. It's a relief; anyone who might look over would notice her first, so I feel safely invisible. She does her thing about three feet away, while I try to find ways to move my limbs that don't feel pointless. I keep waiting for that thing to kick in, that carefree fluidity of motion that I've always gotten on dance floors, but it doesn't come. Sometimes I just copy what she's doing so I won't have to think about it. Mostly we don't make eye contact, but occasionally she catches me mimicking her and flashes me a big smile.

She's being so nice. But the whole thing just makes me sad.

I leave when the song is over. I walk past the squad on purpose. I don't look at them.

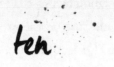

ten

IN THE DRIVEWAY, I PONDER WHETHER TO SNEAK in or not.

It feels weird, wondering this at 9:14 p.m., rather than at four a.m. But Mom very well might be watching TV in the living room, maybe Nick at Nite or killing time before *SNL* comes on. I don't want to talk to her tonight. Still, I would feel ridiculous crawling through my window in my dress at 9:14 p.m., and I wonder if neighbors might see me.

I decide to risk Mom time and come through the front door. The living room is empty. Thank God.

I crash into my room, peeling off this stupid ball gown and stuffing it in the trash. I rub my makeup off, not getting all the eyeliner below my eyes and not caring. I look a little bit Goth like this, like Jack's tiny Morticia Addams friend. What's her name? Andraleia. I look a little like Andraleia.

I feel about 10 percent better.

My phone buzzes. It's Becca, replying-all on the squad group text. **Girl! Did u bounce early? 2 nites in a row?!** with some sad and confused little emoji faces.

Why did she send that on the group text? Why does everyone need to see this? Or is it intentional? Does she want to make sure everyone knows I left early?

Coming down w something. U all look gorj. Dance the night away, and I add some dancing emoji ladies.

I'm amazed that I got a text at all, but now that Becca has reached out, will anyone else? Just to save face? To *act* like they care, like I'm not invisible to them?

Feel better girl, Becca responds with a kissy face, but no one else does. Maybe they're not looking at their phones while they're dancing. Maybe they'll text me later. But I fall asleep with the lights on and I wake up at 3:07 a.m. and I check my phone and no one else has texted me and then I can't get back to sleep.

I suddenly wonder if Heather is on the group text; I don't think she's ever chimed in on it. I check the list, and she's not. She probably doesn't even know there is one.

I hate it when I can't sleep. I always start thinking about the worst things. Nightmares I've had, or horror movies.

Tonight I start thinking about dying. How easy it would be to go into the garage and turn Mom's car on and just not leave. It sounds so peaceful. Just never waking up again.

Then I start thinking about the squad rolling their eyes when they find out, replying-all on the group text, *Ugh so melodramatic.* I think about Raejean telling an incoming sophomore next year, *Yeah, there was another girl on the team, but she offed herself after homecoming. For, like, no reason. SO pathetic.* I think about them faking sadness at my funeral, or just not coming at all. Their moms would send my mom flowers, and someone else would have to do that lift with terrible Evelyn Rice.

My mom would be sad. She'd be the only one, though. She'd also milk it for all it was worth. When Dad left, I remember how she would talk about it with moms she ran into at the grocery store, hand on her heart, the same phrases every time, "I mean *I'll* be fine, but the *chil*dren?!" I imagine her doing the same thing with my death, shaking her head, pursing her lips: *and she was* so *young . . .*

This fantasy is becoming less and less appealing.

Raejean, Raejean, what have you done to me? Did you poison the whole team against me, or did it all just happen together, almost of its own accord? What did I do to deserve this? Am I doomed to spend the next two years alone and friendless? How could I possibly survive that?

And seriously, Becca Ruiz and her fake concern and her group text can eat a bag of dicks. Where have you been the last month? If you're so worried about me, then why couldn't you sit through a whole conversation with me tonight? WHY IS NO ONE LOOKING OUT FOR ME?

I'm crying and crying and crying into my pillow, crying so

hard I'm hyperventilating, and I don't know how to make it stop, so I just keep going and going until I wear myself out.

I've never been bullied. Not really. But it turns out, no one has to shove you in a locker to make you want to die. All they have to do is aggressively not give a shit about you.

eleven

WHEN I WAKE UP, I AM CLEARHEADED AND CALM,
and I know what I want.

I want Raejean Winters to feel pain.

I have no idea what that means yet, and I don't care. In this moment, just knowing the desire is enough. I feel like I'm about ten pounds lighter, even as I feel just a little sick to my stomach. Nervous-excited-scared. It's a hell of an upgrade from the dread that's been sitting on my chest the whole past month.

I walk out to the kitchen. Jack is reading the Sunday comics. "You left early," he says without looking up. "I thought maybe you and Raejean were sneaking off to go to another party or something, but she was still there."

"Raejean kinda sucks right now," I reply. I'm amazed at how my new knowledge—*Raejean Winters must feel pain*—keeps my head level, keeps my heart rate from jumping like it might have just yesterday at the topic of Raejean.

"You guys have a fight?"

"What are you, Mom?" He shrugs, still not looking at me. "Where is she, anyway?"

"Grocery store."

"Don't tell her I left the dance early, okay? I don't wanna deal with Twenty Questions."

"Why would I tell her that?"

I shrug. I motion for him to give me the part of the comics he's not reading, and he hands it over. "I only knew you left early 'cause James told me," he says.

"Who's James?"

"In the tux? You guys danced right before you left?"

My mind goes blank trying to think of guys. I really hadn't danced at all except at the end. "The only person I danced with was your friend Gemma," I say.

"James," he says. "He's trans. It's James now."

I blink at him. "What?"

Jack finally looks up at me and talks slowly, like I'm five. "James is transgender. So don't call him Gemma. It's James."

I just stare back at him, so he keeps explaining, talking even slower now. "Female to male? *Transgender?*"

"But if . . ." I have so many questions but can't seem to formulate any of them. "She . . ."

"*He.* Jesus, Jenna, it's not that hard."

"He . . . used the women's room last night. He asked me to guard the door. I thought he was doing coke or something."

"He probably just wanted to pee standing up without anyone seeing his feet facing the wrong way and getting freaked out."

"But . . . Why was he using the girls' room if . . . ?"

"Well, he's not out to everyone. I just assumed you knew. Mom knows."

"How would I know? I'm not friends with Gemma."

"James."

"James. I don't really know him."

"Well. He definitely doesn't do coke. I don't think he'd know where to get it."

"Oh." I sit down. I feel stupid. "I just thought— He was like really energetic when he came out, and like really insistent on me dancing, so I just thought maybe . . ." I let the sentence die.

Jack goes back to the comics. "James just really likes to dance."

I keep trying to piece it all together. "So he's gonna get the surgery?"

Jack heaves a huge sigh. "Oh my God, Jenna, it is not about the surgery."

"Okay, okay—"

"Other people's genitals are none of your business, okay? He was assigned female at birth, but he's a dude. It's actually very simple."

"I just don't know any other transgender people—"

"Yeah, obviously." He rolls his eyes.

"Is he gonna be okay with me knowing? Should I act like I don't know?"

"Nah. Use his real name. It makes him feel good."

"You mean call him James?"

He gives me the *you're stupid* look again. "Yeah, James. His *real name*."

"Okay."

I get up to get myself a yogurt cup. "Do you do coke?" Jack asks, not looking up.

"Absolutely not."

"I don't judge. I dunno what you cheerleaders do."

"Not coke. Except this one girl last year."

"Probably for the best." He looks up at me again. "The music sucked. You didn't miss much."

Shut up, Jack, you have more friends than I do now. But I just nod and say, "That's good," and take my yogurt back to my room.

twelve

I DON'T KNOW YET WHAT I'M GONNA DO TO HURT Raejean, but I'm just glad to know there's going to be *some*thing. The search for something appropriately painful is a nice reprieve from the endless heartache of the last month, the unreturned texts, the constant trying to fix things. With this one little thought—*I am going to hurt you*—I can let all that go. Drop it off a cliff.

I can tell the difference the next time I walk into practice, too. Lately I've been walking in as though I was going to get pelted with tomatoes, preemptively wincing. But today, on Monday, I walk in with my shoulders down, feeling solitary and free. I exist in a separate bubble from my teammates, floating past them all as I change into my practice clothes.

For some reason, Raejean chooses a locker near me. She hasn't done that in weeks. I'm not thrown by it, though. I even feel strong enough to make small talk.

"How was the rest of the dance," I say, no question mark, like I don't care, because I don't.

"It was pretty good," she replies, and I can tell she's looking at me, but I don't look back. "We went to Denny's afterward."

"Uh-huh."

I sneak a look at her. She's all changed already. She looks nervous, sitting on the bench with her elbows tucked into her sides. I stifle a smile.

"You feeling better?"

Her voice is flat with obligation or pity or something; it's not a real question. A few days ago this would've pissed me off. Now it bounces off me. I just shrug. "Sure."

"Good." She seems like she might say something else, but I get up and walk into the gym before she can.

I am going to hurt you.

Homecoming is over; time to work on our next routine. Not as good as Heather's. It doesn't matter. I throw myself into the new moves as hard as I can. Kick my leg up as high as I can, point my toe as hard as I can, jump in the air as hard as I can. Even when we're supposed to be just marking the moves, I perform full out, and Coach Mason says, "Good, Jenna," and I pretend I don't hear her because I'm concentrating *that hard*. White-hot rage becomes white-hot focus, and I fall into a sort of trance, letting the rhythm guide me through the moves. Coach gives us a quick water break, but I keep practicing, eyes glued to the mirror. I look good. I feel good.

In the mirror, I see Raejean starting to redo her French

braid, then letting Meghan take over. That used to be my job, smell of Herbal Essences shampoo wafting up from her long blond waves kept obsessively free of split ends, folding the sections into each other carefully. Meghan says something I can't hear, and Raejean laughs.

I am going to hurt you.

I push everyone out of my head. Focus on the moves, focus on the moves.

Afterward, she doesn't try to make conversation again, and neither do I. I feel calm, letting the waves of endorphins drown out the noise in my head. I can tell I pushed myself harder today. Maybe this is how hard I should have been working this whole time. Maybe that's the only way to survive this year.

I blast the music in my car before I've even gotten out of the parking lot. Evelyn Rice, still waiting at the curb for her mom, jumps at the sudden sound; I just smile. I catch a flicker of Raejean in my rearview mirror as I pull away. She's not looking at me.

I am going to hurt you.

At home, I make lists.

Things that are important to Raejean Winters:
- NOT ME
- Her mom
- Her weight
- Marcus Carlsberg
- Meghan
- Being the best gymnast on the team

- *Her health*
- *Her grades*
- *Being pretty*

Then, right next to it:

Ways I could sabotage:
- *Tell her mom she's smoking pot (she might then rat me out, too—no good)*
- *Somehow make her fat (no clue how to do this)*
- *Seduce Marcus somehow (he's never met me, only entry point is through Meghan)*
- *Become Meghan's best friend, then talk shit about Raejean (too time-intensive)*
- *Get her thrown off the team (for what?)*
- *Give her mono (how?)*
- *Steal an important paper out of her bag and make her fail a class (no good, she'd have a backup on her computer)*
- *"Accidentally" scar her face*

The last one seems the most feasible, but I still have no idea how to pull it off. When I think about actually scarring her face, when I think about looking at a bandage or a scab or a streak of scar tissue in the middle of her porcelain-smooth face, my stomach tightens and I want to cry.

I slam my journal shut and put on the music for our routine, running the moves in my head.

At practice and games, I ignore her. She ignores me. At lunch, she whispers with Meghan Finnegan and giggles too loudly. She thinks her laugh is adorable, but really it's just obnoxious. It sounds like a machine gun. *I am going to hurt you.*

I stop watching her. I watch myself in the mirror, I "engage my core" and push my leg higher and higher and higher in the air. I look good—or, at least, I look flexible; Coach keeps having to remind me to smile. When other girls stretch with each other, when Melissa and Evelyn or Meghan and Raejean sit spread-eagle across from each other and pull each other into a perfect 180 with their legs, I stretch by myself, doing center splits until my crotch hits the floor.

My form has never been better. I wish that was enough to make me not want to die.

I am going to hurt you.

Every morning when I wake up before practice, I consider staying in bed. If I could just be asleep, I wouldn't have to deal with this storm cloud of dread that I walk around in now. Instead I hop up and do push-ups in the dark. That's when *I am going to hurt you* pushes my body, makes me work harder. Other times *I am going to hurt you* gets drowned out by the strain and the sweat and the feeling of my pulse pounding in my ears, before surging back at top volume.

I am going to hurt you. I am going to hurt you. What if I didn't? What if I didn't hurt you, Raejean? What if I let this whole thing go? (But how do I do that, exactly? How do I stop hating you?)

A week of this goes by, then two, then three. The football

season starts winding down. I wait for *I am going to hurt you* to dissipate. It doesn't.

I hate you so much, Raejean, but I would take you back in a second. If you would just text me and ask me what's up, I know that everything would go back to normal. I also know you're not going to do that.

I am going to hurt you.

I wish I wasn't.

thirteen

AFTER GAMES, I TAKE MYSELF STRAIGHT HOME,
skipping the after-parties and group hangs—not that I'm being
invited anymore. I am, presumably, removed from the ongoing
group text.

We learn our competition routine, which we will be performing over and over until approximately February. A competition routine has to have certain tricks and moves—this many
basket tosses, this many tumbling sections—and is just way
more generic. No room for creativity. Ours ends with Raejean
hoisted high in the air; I'm a base, with her foot in my hand. She
looks like a statue, or the angel on top of a Christmas tree.

As a rule, we *slay* at competitions. The first one is in San
Luis Obispo, the second weekend of November—just a couple
of weeks away now. Honestly, none of us take San Luis Obispo
seriously. It's a competition that gives awards to everyone, based

on your score: over an eighty-five is a silver, over a ninety-two is a gold. We've *always* gotten the gold. But an easy win is still a win.

Halloween comes and goes. Jack goes trick-or-treating with Andraleia, James (I feel guilty whenever I call him Gemma in my mind), Karissa, and Axel. They've all dressed as the Avengers; Mom takes a group photo in our living room. I have no costume, and I stay home.

The plan is to all drive up to San Luis Obispo, caravan style. Due to a snafu long before my time where a girl accidentally got left behind for a competition, Coach designates who goes in what car, despite our pleas to the contrary every year.

My heart stops when I see the e-mail. My car: Raejean, Evelyn, and Melissa.

Shit.

Mom desperately wants to come, like she did last year; I beg her not to at dinner one night while Jack is at Axel's. "We've got enough cars. And you'd have to get your own hotel room, and I know you're trying to save money right now." The last thing I need is my mom snuggling up to me while the rest of the squad steadfastly ignores me. Plus, upperclassmen with their own cars don't bring their moms. It's just not done.

"I save money so I can do things like this," she says with a smirk.

"But it's San Luis Obispo; it's not even an important competition. If you're gonna drive for five hours it should be for a competition that actually matters."

She purses her lips. "What do you girls do up there that you're so eager for me not to see?"

86

"Nothing, Mom, Jesus. We do each other's hair and stuff. Why would anyone drink right before a competition? That makes no sense."

"I didn't say drinking, you said drinking. Is there drinking?"

"No, Mom, there's no freaking drinking!"

"You know, maybe I do wanna come after all. You're making this all sound so fun, sweetie." She crosses her arms and smiles. I can tell she's enjoying ribbing me, but she also seems somewhat serious. Maybe she might invite herself along after all.

I've gotten so heated up and frustrated that I can feel my face filling up with tears, and rather than fight them, I decide to just let them out in front of her. She sits up straight and starts rubbing my back. "Oh, honey, what's wrong?"

I scramble for the right lie. "You just . . . never trust me, no matter what I do, no matter how hard I work, it's never enough, you don't trust me . . ." She sits there quietly rubbing my back; I don't dare look at her face, in case she sees the lie on mine.

"Now, that is not true at all. I think I show you quite a bit of trust, especially compared with when I was growing up." I sniffle and wipe my eyes, still not looking at her.

"It's just . . . really important to me to do this on my own," I whimper.

She sighs. "If you're going to do this—and I haven't said yes yet—you need to keep on top of things around here. No dishes left in the sink, no hair clogging the shower, done with homework and in bed by eleven. Okay?"

I throw my arms around her, heart pounding. "Thank you thank you thank you."

"And if I find out there has been even a *sip* of alcohol in that hotel room—"

"You won't."

"You will be so grounded."

"Won't happen. I promise." I kiss her on the cheek and run to my room.

———————

On Friday, the day before the competition, we all meet up in the parking lot after school: Coach, the squad, and a few parents who are driving up with us. Meghan and Raejean have their arms around each other, singing Katy Perry at the top of their lungs. I hear Meghan plead with Coach, "Can't Raejean please come in my car?" Coach ignores her, handing out printouts with elaborate driving directions to all the drivers, as though we weren't all just going to use the GPS on our phones anyway.

It's a five-hour drive to San Luis Obispo *without* traffic, but leaving on a Friday afternoon means we're going to hit rush hour. I am not looking forward to this.

Evelyn and Melissa insist on sitting together in the back seat, which gives Raejean shotgun. She doesn't say a word for the first hour of the journey, while Evelyn and Melissa chatter away; I tune them out.

Eventually we get far enough out of town that the Top 40 changes to static, hovering at the edge of my attention while

I focus on not hitting cars or looking at Raejean. She starts to plug my audio cable into her phone. "What are you doing?!" I snap at her.

"Putting on music," she replies, pushing buttons. I pull the cable away.

"You don't change the music without asking. That's just bad etiquette," I say, and I can feel her eyes saying, *Since when?*

"There was no music. It was just static," she says.

"You just. Ask first. It's standard."

She crosses her arms and says nothing. The static on the radio continues. I grab the cable and plug it into my phone. "That's literally exactly what I was doing," she mutter-whispers.

"What was that?" I ask her, loud. She shakes her head and says nothing. I put on a playlist and try to pretend I'm enjoying the music.

I look to my back-seat passengers in the rearview mirror. "How you guys doing back there?" I ask, like I'm my mom. Melissa gives me a thin, unconvincing smile. No one says anything.

After another ten minutes or so, Evelyn Rice leans forward and pokes her head between the front seats. "Raejean, how's it all going with *Marcus*?"

Right. Marcus Carlsberg, German Foreign Exchange Student. How *is* that all going, Raejean?

She immediately perks up and laughs. "Oh my God. He's so ridiculous."

"Why is he ridiculous?"

"We had this whole conversation where he got all freaked

out about what he would tell his mom about me, and I'm like, dude, you don't live here, not trying to marry you, I'm literally just trying to make out with your face."

Melissa pokes her head in, too: "Is he a good kisser?"

"He's like. *Fine.* I think he does too much tongue. Which I tried to explain, but I think there was a language barrier?"

I can't believe I'm finding out all this from a conversation Raejean is having with *Evelyn Rice.* Evelyn who we used to make fun of! Back at cheer camp, we would take turns doing impressions of Evelyn's nasal voice: *Can you* just? *Explain the move* again? *So I'm sure I've* got *it?* Now they're bonding over Marcus Carlsberg. How is this my life right now?

I sneak a look at Raejean in the passenger seat, with the sunlight hitting her face just so, her wavy golden hair falling so perfectly around her shoulders like always.

The three of them chatter on, ignoring me until I pull off for gas.

fourteen

AT DINNER THAT NIGHT, I REMAIN IGNORED, EXCEPT by Coach. "Jenna, sit by me." We've pushed a bunch of tables together at the Olive Garden, sitting in one long row, with me and Coach in the corner.

I avoid eye contact as I pick at the unlimited salad.

"How's your mom doing, Jenna?"

"She's fine."

"I was surprised not to see her here."

"Well, now that I can drive myself . . ."

"Right. Right." Coach blows on her minestrone soup. "Tell her I say hi."

"I will."

At the other end of the table, Meghan slips an ice cube down the back of Raejean's shirt, and Raejean shrieks; then they both start laughing convulsively. Why is an ice cube okay, but a glass of water wasn't?

I'm so tired. I let myself just space out, watching Raejean and Meghan grabbing each other and giggling uncontrollably. I am so tired. I am so tired of this. I'm just so tired.

Later, in our hotel room, with Coach and the parents off in their own rooms, we all sit on the floor and play Ten Fingers, all starting with our hands out and all ten fingers pointing toward the ceiling, like we're getting ready to slap each other ten. "Never have I ever given a blow job." "Never have I ever gotten so drunk I threw up." "Never have I ever cheated on a test." If we've done the thing, we put down a finger; if we were drinking, we'd also take a sip (but, true to my word to my mom, we're not tonight); and if you're the only one who's done it, you have to tell the story.

When it gets to Raejean, she thinks for a moment and then giggles. "Never have I ever . . . shit my pants since I was five."

Go to hell, Raejean.

She knows—she *knows* that that time I had food poisoning when I was thirteen was utterly humiliating. She promised at the time never to tell anyone. She *knows* that. Why would she choose that one?! How dare she bring that up?!

I decide simply not to put a finger down. No one puts a finger down.

Raejean stares at me, her brow furrowed. Her face says, *You know this one applies to you. Put the finger down.*

I just stare back. *No. And fuck you.*

92

Is she going to say anything? There's an epic silence in the room.

She looks around at the group, smiling. "No one? It's okay. You can admit it." But no one moves.

Finally, Meghan sitting next to her says, "Never have I ever broken a bone."

The game continues. Raejean goes back to ignoring me. But I just keep glaring at her, my face growing hotter and hotter.

Fine. Raejean, you brought this on yourself. You could have avoided this so easily. You could have talked to me or apologized or at least tried to be friendly. You could have, at the *very least*, not tried to blow up my spot about shitting myself when I was thirteen. You had so many chances. You could so easily have made a billion different choices. But you didn't.

So, fine. If this is where it all ends up, then this is where it all ends up.

I am going to hurt you. Tonight.

fifteen

I DON'T KNOW WHAT I'M GOING TO DO YET, BUT I know that no one else can be awake when I do it.

I set my alarm for two a.m., a silent vibrating alarm so no one else will hear it, but it turns out I don't need it; I can't sleep. I lie in bed with my stomach bunched up, staring at the red numbers on the alarm clock, trying to breathe. Trying to wait until as close to two as possible so that I know for sure that people are asleep.

At sleepovers, I always used to be the last one asleep. When I'm at home in my bed, I fall right to sleep, but at sleepovers I'd be worried about missing something, so I would stay up even past when everyone else had drifted off and even then not want to go to sleep.

Part of me legitimately wants to kill her. I let the images fly through my mind: her shocked eyes as I pull a gun on her, right before I pull the trigger, or the satisfying feeling of sinking the blade of a pair of scissors into her chest. The images pass.

1:22.

What if I don't do it? What if I just turn off my alarm and close my eyes right now and never do anything? What if I let this be where all these thoughts end tonight?

No. No. Just entertaining the idea feels like tucking my tail between my legs, like folding myself up inside a tiny cardboard box, holding still so I fit inside. Am I going to just let her get away with the way she's treated me? Am I going to just keep going on like this while nothing changes? I can't, I can't, I can't.

1:32. Everyone's breathing is even and soft. They all must be asleep, right?

We're three to a bed, plus girls with sleeping bags on the floor; there are other girls in the neighboring hotel room, but Raejean is here, squeezed in with Meghan and Becca. I'm on the floor right next to her.

I get up very, very slowly and start snooping around. I don't even know what I'm looking for. What if I put her hand in warm water so she pisses herself? That'd be a nice payback for tonight. (No, then she'd get it on Meghan, and somehow everyone would be mad at *me* even though Raejean would be the one wetting the bed.)

I gently lift the lids of other girls' suitcases, but I don't see anything I could use for sabotage, and I'm worried that if I start digging, someone will hear me.

No one's watching, right? I look around; everyone's asleep. Then Ebony moves her foot, and I nearly yelp out loud.

I shut myself in the bathroom to calm down. And to give myself plausible deniability in case anyone does wake up. I take deep breaths.

My eyes land on Raejean's cosmetics kit. The pale pink zip-up lunchbox-looking thing that her mom got her last Christmas. I zip it open, hovering my fingers over palettes of eyeshadow and blush.

Should I toss her makeup in the toilet? No, she'd just borrow from someone else. It has to be bigger than that.

My eyes land on her manicure set. Cuticle pushers, nail clippers—and scissors, deceptively sharp scissors, scissors of such an improbably large size that we laughed when she got the kit, because who needs scissors that big to cut their nails? She'd used them mostly to trim her split ends.

I pick up the scissors and poke the tip gently with my finger.

I know I can't *cut* her. I can't use these on her skin, any fantasies about scarring her face notwithstanding. That's too far. Plus she'd wake up and scream or something. I guess I don't really have a use for these.

But just as I'm about to set them down, my eyes land on her shampoo and conditioner.

Of course.

How many nights did I spend perched on the edge of the tub while she conditioned her wavy blond hair with avocado and mayonnaise? How many hundreds of hours?

We're all supposed to have a uniform look as a team at competitions, so we all slick our hair up into ponytails with a big bow. Even Ebony, who prefers to wear her hair natural, straightens her hair for competitions so we all have the same ponytail.

It would take so little movement. I could even do it from my sleeping bag.

Don't do it. You can't undo it once you've done it. But I can't not do anything, either. Not after that round of Ten Fingers.

I feel like I'm going to vomit.

I tuck the scissors into the waistband of my pants and zip up Raejean's cosmetics kit. I wonder if I should flush the toilet, for the plausible-deniability factor, but I decide not to risk waking anyone up. I open the bathroom door quietly; everyone is still.

I return to my sleeping bag, making as little noise as possible, and reach for my waistband. I wrap my hand around the scissors. They're so cold. Slowly I pull them out, and just as slowly I sit up.

It's dark. The curtains are drawn. No one would be able to tell what these are right now anyway, right?

My heart is pounding so, so hard, and my hands are shaking, and I'm worried that I'll slip and nick her with the scissors and wake her up.

From several sleeping bags over, Heather shifts in her sleep, and I freeze. Is she waking up? I sit as still as possible, and I wait, and I wait. Nothing. I take a chance and whisper her name. "Heather?"

Nothing.

I take a long inhale. I inch closer to Raejean's bed. She's sleeping on her side with her back to me, her ponytail lying prone on the pillowcase. It's almost too perfect.

Is this a trap? Did she somehow know I would try this? Is she just pretending to be asleep?

I watch the little movements of her body from the floor, her shoulders shifting just the tiniest bit with each breath. I know what Raejean asleep looks like; I've seen it a million times. I know that she couldn't fake this. I know that I'd have to shake her, hard, to wake her up right now. But I hesitate just the same. *Of course she's asleep. Don't be an idiot.*

Her ponytail is loose enough that I can cut right under the band and take it all off at once.

My stomach starts shaking, and tears come out of my eyes. I am completely silent even as I cry. Jesus, Jenna, so dramatic. So weak. I wipe my eyes.

Just make it all stop. Just make everything stop, for one second. Just make it stop.

Slowly, slowly I reach up and cut into her ponytail. It takes three big snips, and the whole thing comes off in one neat piece. Her perfect blond mane, gone. The amputated ponytail lies on her pillow, separate, elegant.

I look around. No one is awake.

I've pulled it off. I've done it. I feel light and giddy. I've done it, I've done it, I've done it. I've done it! Oh my God! I—

Wait. *Shit.* I'm right next to her bed! Everyone is going to know I did it, because how could someone have cut her hair without climbing over me?

SHIT.

I wiggle my sleeping bag as far from the bed as I can without

98

bumping into anyone else. I still look suspicious, but at least there's, conceivably, some walking room where someone could have snuck in and done the job.

And—SHIT. What do I do with these scissors?! Now I have to go back to the bathroom after all this and risk waking someone up? Shit, shit, *shit*. I start looking around for places to hide them. In a drawer? No, they'll look in the drawers. Won't they? What am I talking about? I have to put them back in Raejean's kit. Nothing can be out of place.

I tuck the scissors into my waistband again and wiggle out of my sleeping bag; the scissors poke me in the hip as I stand up, and I bite my lip to keep from screaming. I pad over to the bathroom, not even closing the door this time for fear the sound will startle someone. Shit, shit—my fingerprints are all over these now! I rub the scissors down with a towel and drop them in the process; my heart stops, but they land on the bath mat without a sound. I grab a washcloth, pick up the scissors, replace them in Raejean's kit, and zip it up again.

What have I done? Oh my God. Why did I think this was a good idea? In the morning there'll be a witch hunt, and everyone will know it was me. What have I done? Oh God, oh God, oh God, what is wrong with me? *What the hell is wrong with me?*

I skitter back to my sleeping bag and lie down, slamming my eyes shut. Go to sleep right now. Go to sleep right this minute and make sure you are asleep when they find this out.

Will Raejean scream? Will she cry? None of these thoughts give me any pleasure whatsoever. Oh God oh God.

Maybe I could just leave. If I grab my things quietly and drive home right now, I won't have to see how this plays out. No one would be able to see my face in the morning, see my reaction. *But of course then they'd know it was you. There would be no doubt.* If I drive away, I drive away forever. Maybe that's okay?

I can't will myself to move. I lie there with my cheek to my pillow, turned away from Raejean's bed, and keep my eyes squeezed shut. *Go to sleep, go to sleep, go to sleep right now.*

But I can't. I lie there and listen to the raging drum solo in my chest. I let my eyes fall open and look at the red numbers on the alarm clock: 2:02.

My phone is buzzing—my alarm. I hadn't even heard it. I turn the alarm off and close my eyes and pray for sleep that doesn't come, startling at every single shift and breath and rustle.

sixteen

WHEN I WAKE UP, I HAVE A FEW PEACEFUL MOMENTS before I realize what I've done, before I remember where I am or what's happening. Then it all slams back to me in a rush, and amid the sinking in my stomach, I'm also amazed: How did I ever fall asleep after all that?

I stay in my sleeping bag with my eyes closed and listen for the chaos that I'm sure must be ensuing. Is everyone in a panic? Are they searching all our bags, dusting for fingerprints? Is there screaming, crying, hysteria?

I listen. Nothing. Well, not *nothing*. I can hear the running of the shower, the zipping and rustling and rolling of suitcases being packed and unpacked. I hear whispering, the words of which I can't make out. I crack my eye open just a slit, sneaking a look at the clock: 9:27 a.m.

Was last night a fever dream? Did I really do what I think

I did? I let my gaze fall on Raejean's bed; it's empty. Maybe none of it really happened. Maybe I'm having a psychotic break.

I sit up and look around. No one is looking at me. That's good, isn't it? Or is it?

Raejean is nowhere to be found. Neither is Meghan.

I can feel my hands shaking. I get up and roll up my sleeping bag as casually as possible, focusing on keeping my breathing steady. I look around at the room. Everyone is going about their business, same as always. No one seems angry or afraid or unnerved.

What is happening? Aren't we all supposed to be freaking out right now?

I wait my turn for the shower, try to scrub the guilt out of my skin, feeling especially guilty as I wash my hair. The hot water makes my heart beat even faster.

Jodi asks me as I come out of the shower if I know where Raejean and Meghan are. "We thought they went down to breakfast, but my mom says they're not there." I shrug and shake my head. She buries her face in her phone.

Shit shit shit shit shit.

I put on my gear, pack my bag. As I open our hotel door, Raejean and Meghan are standing there facing me, key card in hand.

Raejean's hair has clearly been trimmed, shaped, styled into a pixie cut; she looks elfin. It's abrupt, she definitely looked better with long hair, but it still works. Of course it still works; she's gorgeous. But the look in her eyes as we stand facing each other is unmistakable hatred.

It only lasts a moment; then she breaks into a smile and breezes past me. Meghan doesn't look at me as she follows. One by one, the girls in the room see Raejean. Some of them squeal; some of them just let their jaws drop. "Hey, ladies," Raejean says breezily.

"Raejean, *what*?" Becca is touching Raejean's scalp and neck. "Why in the hell did you get your hair cut at nine in the morning?" Everyone is crowded around her, cooing and gasping. I just stand there in the doorway like a dumb deer.

"I got gum in it," Raejean laughs. "I fell asleep with gum in my mouth, and when I woke up it was in my hair."

"Baby, there are *so many ways* to get gum out of hair without cutting it!" Becca says, shaking her head.

"I know. I just panicked and made Meghan take me to the only hair salon that was open."

"Supercuts," Meghan says with a smile. "At that big mall we passed?"

"Although honestly, I'd been thinking about getting it cut like this for a while."

Jodi is running her fingers through Raejean's hair and giggling. "It looks so good!"

"Yeah, I'm really happy with how it came out." Raejean preens like she's on the red carpet.

"Coach is gonna be *pissed*, though," Evelyn Rice pipes up.

"Yeah, I'll deal with Coach," Raejean says, adjusting her new hair in the mirror on the wall.

"Can you still put a bow in it?" Jodi asks.

As the other girls fuss over Raejean's hair, I quietly finish my exit and make my way down the hall toward the elevator, heart in my throat.

This makes no sense. Why would Raejean say the haircut was her idea? At the very least, Meghan knows it isn't. My heart leaps: Is Raejean trying to protect me? Does she still, after everything, want to keep me out of trouble? Did I underestimate our friendship?

As I reach into my purse for my key card, my hand lands on something soft: Raejean's ponytail, still in its black band, lying at the bottom of my bag.

I didn't put it there.

seventeen

I SIT AT THE BREAKFAST BUFFET BY MYSELF, SIPPING
orange juice and sweating. It's nearly ten a.m. I consult the
printed schedule Coach handed out; we're due to be at the convention center in an hour.

My purse is closed, but I just know someone is going to see
inside it. Or someone will see a single long, blond hair hanging
off the zipper, and they'll know. Everyone is going to know.

What if I just go to the lobby bathroom and flush it? Or
would it back up the toilet? What if someone else saw it in the
bottom of the bowl? I stay put.

Girls don't so much sit down with me as spring up around
me, chatting over my head and past me, laughing too loudly. It's
too early. Don't they know it's too early to be so loud?

I've deliberately chosen a seat as far from Coach as possible,
and when Raejean comes in with Meghan, I see Coach's eyes

widen. She stands and marches directly to Raejean. I can't make out exactly what she's saying, but she is not happy.

Raejean whispers something in Coach's ear, and Coach's whole body changes. Her posture goes from anger to shock. Raejean whispers something else, and Coach nods. Is it just me, or do her eyes land on me for a brief moment?

Coach nods, pats Raejean on the back, and motions for her to get something to eat. Raejean gives Coach a watery smile and sets her bag down on a chair, never looking at me once.

I don't know what's going to happen, but I can tell that today is going to be terrible.

After breakfast, Raejean rides with Meghan to the convention center. Jodi rides shotgun with me instead. The car is silent the whole way.

It's a struggle to keep my eyes open as we wait for Coach to wade through registration, as we make our way to the fluorescent-lit mirror-walled warm-up room, as we stretch on the bright blue mats. I should've gotten coffee at breakfast.

As we sit in the bleachers watching the other routines, there is no doubt that some of our hive mind is still there.

That girl came out of her toe touch a little hard; I bet that hurt. No one says it, but we all clock it and wince together. *Those two got out of sync on their back handsprings. Looks like their coach didn't do them any favors; it takes longer to set up their stunts than it does to do them. That girl's not flexible enough to do a good scorpion—why'd they make her a flyer? Ugh, their school's colors are orange and brown? I feel so sorry for them.*

We see it. Sometimes we say it, but we don't need to. We all know it. I can tell from how our torsos lift and contract and from the moment when someone puts her hand over her mouth or sucks in her breath. We all see the same thing.

It used to be like this all the time, with everything. I miss that so much.

Everyone seems to be thinking about the other acts and not about Raejean and her hair—even Raejean. She's clipped her bow to the top of her head, and it looks a bit ridiculous, but no one seems to notice. This should be a relief, but it feels like a trap.

I'm sorry, I'm sorry, I'm sorry.

After about an hour of watching the other routines, Coach gives us a small nod. "Ladies, you're on deck." We nod back. "You got this. Remember that you are one unit. Keep your awareness of each other at all times." Some girls' moms hug and kiss them and wish them luck. We make our way through the labyrinth of hallways to backstage. Some teams' coaches go backstage with them; ours stays in the bleachers. "I want to see what the judges see," she's told us. "At this point my work is done."

There are five routines ahead of us. Squads are stretching, running through as many of the moves as they can do in the cramped space. Occasionally, rogue male cheerleaders will whisper and laugh with their female teammates. A lot of the other teams are amped up, giggly, helping each other to stretch or mark through lifts together. Ours is somber, silently stretching and avoiding eye contact.

At two routines till go time, Mandy Lockley assembles us into a circle, and we do a hands-in. "Go, Puffins," we whisper, without exclamation point, without joy, and we wordlessly make our way into line so we can come out in the correct formation, Raejean right behind me. I focus hard on the team onstage, what I can see of them from the wings. Despite their loud techno music, it feels completely silent backstage.

Raejean leans forward and presses her nose against the top of my ear.

"I know it was you," she whispers. "I could tell everyone that it was you."

I hold my breath. I meekly shake my head no.

"You don't care if you ruin it for all of us."

I blink back white-hot tears and stand very still.

"Don't you dare try anything out there. Don't you dare."

She pulls away from me, and I immediately start running through the routine in my head as hard as I can, trying to push that conversation away. Don't think about it, don't think about it, don't let her get in your head. You've got a job to do. Don't think about it. *Prep and toe touch, prep back handspring . . .*

Arlington High School hits their final pose to whoops and applause. We're next.

In a way it's good that it's Raejean who has the short hair. If someone is going to have to stick out, have it be your flyer. It's not so bad, really. Is it?

Nope, stop thinking about it. Do your job, Jenna.

We skip onto the stage, rustling pom-poms and smiling ear

to ear. I forgot to do my usual whitening strips morning ritual on my teeth this morning; I can't imagine it's actually made a noticeable difference. Parents and Coach and some of the more polite teams cheer for us.

Coach has choreographed this routine to within an inch of its life. Every time a stunt dismounts, a new one goes up at the same time to distract the audience's eye. Toe-touch basket toss after cupie after heel-stretch extension, bam, bam, bam. It's a barrage of sensory overload to watch. Onstage, we can't even be thinking about anyone else's stunts but our own. Everything's been timed out with the music.

I do not want to do the final stunt, Raejean's big moment. I do not want to stand there with her sneaker in my hand, arms locked, standing between her and the ground.

The moves come automatically, a Pavlovian response to the music, the dubstep sound soup. Everything is timing out perfectly, like always. I feel wooden, like a foreigner in my own body, but the moves are happening and the crowd is cheering. It doesn't give me the high that it usually does, but at least it brings me the memory of that high. I stretch my smile wider, like an animal baring her teeth.

In an isolated snapshot, I see Raejean's bow fly out of her hair and sail offstage. She keeps dancing like she doesn't notice. Maybe she doesn't.

I feel like I'm blacking out or something, like I keep arriving at a new moment in the routine without knowing how I got there. I breathe and try to focus on the moves.

Prep and toe touch, prep back handspring . . .

I hear the weird foghorn in the music that signifies the last stunt of the routine. Raejean faces me with nary a flicker in her eye, all adrenaline and hopped-up team spirit. I take her right foot; Heather takes her left; Meghan spots her. Raejean stands above our heads and swings her left leg up into her left hand, lifting her leg up until her legs are in a perfect 180. Her weight is in my hands. I focus on keeping my arms straight and solid.

I know it was you.

I try to push the thought away, but Raejean has shifted her weight back just a tiny bit, and as I try to adjust, I let my left arm bend the tiniest bit, and then her weight all goes into my left arm, and my elbow buckles—

And Raejean comes crashing to the floor, a backward swan dive in slow motion. Meghan catches her and cushions her fall, but Raejean's right foot lands on the floor sickeningly hard, and she lets out an animal yelp-howl that I've never heard, before slipping out of Meghan's arms and crumpling all the way down to the floor.

The music has stopped. For a moment there's just silence. Some girls, standing in front of the stunt, hold their pose and wait for the applause, not wanting to break character to investigate the pandemonium behind them. Then suddenly there's the *whoosh* of *ohhhh*s and concerned noises from the audience. A gray-haired stage-manager woman in all black rushes out from backstage and kneels by Raejean's side. "Can you get up? Do we need to call an ambulance?"

Raejean doesn't answer her. She looks up at me with her jaw hanging slack and her eyes wide, shaking her head the tiniest bit, and I know what she's thinking.

"No," I say. "No no no no no, I wouldn't." And I shake my head *no* emphatically, *of course I didn't do this on purpose*, but she's not looking at me anymore, she's lying there like a wounded bird, and I hear her say to the stage-manager woman that she thinks she does need an ambulance.

She looks so small and pale with her short hair and her big eyes, and she winces with the pain as tears run down her face. I try to go to her side, but the woman in black holds up a hand to me, says that none of us should touch her right now. I try to ignore the warning, to kneel down next to Raejean anyway, but she recoils from me and turns her head away.

I back off.

I watch as our teammates stand cluelessly to the side, as concerned adults rush in, as Coach talks quietly with the woman in black. I watch Raejean's pale and terrified face. *But isn't this what you wanted?* a voice in my mind says. *To see her brought down? To see her weak and scared?* And I find myself shaking my head again.

No. No. I never ever wanted this at all.

eighteen

RAEJEAN IS VERY CAREFULLY MOVED BACKSTAGE
so the other teams can keep performing, and soon the ambulance arrives. She's stopped crying by the time they get there, and I even see her smile a little at an EMT's joke, which I can't hear. I have the briefest flicker of a thought: *Is she faking it?* But I think about her scared, pale face looking up at me from the floor, and I know that she couldn't have faked that.

Coach brings the girls with cars over and gives us directions to follow the ambulance to the hospital, but before I turn to go, she stops me and leans in close to my face. "Is everything all right?"

I just look up at her, confused. How could everything be all right?

"Is there anything I should know about?"

I just keep staring at her. "Like what?" I ask.

She stares back at me, as though she's looking through my face, and I know that I'm blushing, but I can't make sense of anything she's asked me. She asks me again, calm: "Is there anything I should know about?"

I start to cry and just shake my head no over and over. Coach sighs. "You gotta lock those arms, Jenna," she says. "This is what happens when you don't lock those arms."

"I'm sorry, I'm sorry . . ."

"I know you're sorry. It's a big deal." She gives me that piercing look again. "But accidents happen, right?"

I just nod. I suddenly remember Raejean and Coach's whispered conversation in the hotel lobby; a burning feeling ripples across my back, my arms; I remember that the blond ponytail is still lying at the bottom of my purse. Is Coach going to ask to search me, or . . . ?

But she just turns and walks away.

My mind spins, thinking of my journal back home. Is someone going to go through my room, looking for evidence? Did I put anything in there about wanting to kill her? (*Don't we all want to kill our best friends sometimes?* I imagine myself saying to a judge.) Am I going to be arrested for assault? What if she can never cheer again? What if she can never walk again?

In the hospital waiting room, I text my mom and tell her that there's been an injury and I don't know how long we'll be here. I don't tell her that the injury was Raejean's. I don't tell her that I was the one who caused it. I ignore her replies.

I look around. Everyone is buried in their phones. Occasionally girls whisper to each other, but no one says anything out loud. I bite a hangnail off my ring finger, and my finger bleeds; I stick it in my mouth to stop the bleeding.

I never ever wanted this to happen. Well, I might have briefly imagined Raejean getting hurt, but isn't that normal? Isn't that to be expected? Imagining it doesn't mean I willed it into existence. Does it?

How distraught should I look? If I look too upset, will it be suspicious? But won't it be more suspicious if I'm not upset enough? I look around again; everyone's faces are blank and numb. I try to go for that with my face.

No one has told me, *It wasn't your fault.* I know that it *was* my fault, but I'm kind of annoyed that no one has even tried to tell me it wasn't. I think of Coach's piercing glare: "Accidents happen, right?" Does every single person here think I did this on purpose?

After an hour or so, a doctor talks to Coach, who talks to us. She uses phrases like "torn ankle ligament" and "third-degree sprain" and "thankfully not a fracture." Jodi asks if any of the rest of us can go in and see her, and Coach replies, "She's not feeling up to that right now."

She tells us that it could have been a lot worse. She tells us that Raejean's parents are on their way up to San Luis Obispo. She tells us that we are welcome to drive back home, and that she and Meghan will stay here at the hospital with Raejean.

Normally, we'd stay for the evening awards ceremony, driving home afterward and getting home at something like two a.m. (though some girls' parents occasionally spring for a second night at the hotel). But no one protests the change in plans.

In the car, Evelyn and Melissa stay together in the back seat, leaving the front seat open, like I'm their chauffeur. After about twenty minutes of silence, Evelyn starts laughing quietly to herself. "Wow," she says. "You must feel so bad."

I can't tell if she's trying to be nice or not. "I do," I say. "I really really do."

There's silence again; then she replies, "We've never not gotten the gold at that one, right?"

Her clone, Melissa, sighs dramatically. "Ev, shut *up*."

"It's just a question."

I let the just-question hang in the air. I put on music.

Eventually they start talking about something else, and I have never been so relieved to hear Evelyn's nasal little voice.

My mom pounces on me as soon as I walk in the door. "I saw on Facebook that it was Raejean who got hurt! Oh, honey." She wraps her arms around me. "I know you wish you could've stayed there with her, but you did the right thing, taking the other girls home."

I stand there with my head lying on her shoulder, trying to mentally transport myself to the headspace my mom thinks I'm in right now. "I'm kind of in shock, and I wanna lie down," I say.

"Oh, honey. How bad is it? I'm so sorry."

"I just wanna lie down," I say again. I extricate myself from her embrace as kindly as I can and shut my bedroom door behind me.

The minute I flop down on my bed, I remember how badly I slept last night, and though I am riddled with adrenaline and worry, I fall asleep for four hours.

When I wake up, we all have an e-mail from Coach. Raejean is on her way back home with her mother; she won't be able to cheer for at least two months; and despite the accident, our team still won a silver medal. **Congratulations on the excellence of your form throughout the rest of the routine,** Coach writes.

In Coach's ten years leading the team, this is our first time ever not getting the gold at San Luis Obispo.

Before I can think too hard about it, I'm sitting at my desk and pounding out a reply to the e-mail.

Dear Coach,

While Raejean's accident today was just that—an accident—I do feel responsible for it. I was the one whose arms buckled, so it's my fault. I cost us not only the competition, but Raejean's performance ability.

Given how I've caused harm to the team, I think it's best if I resign. I've violated my teammates' trust, and I think my absence will help everyone to heal and move forward. Please consider this my resignation letter, with my apologies for every-thing I've done.

It has been such a pleasure to be part of this team. Thank you for everything.

Sincerely,

Jenna Watson

I hit Send before I can change my mind and suddenly feel light and heavy all at once. *It's done. It's done. It's really done. The nightmare is over.*

Within two minutes, Coach has sent me a one-line reply:

Come see me about this before practice on Monday.

nineteen

WHEN I WALK INTO COACH'S WINDOWLESS OFFICE,
she's staring at her computer screen, and she doesn't look up at
me. "Jenna. Have a seat." I do. I sit and wait, gazing at the pictures
of Coach and her wife adorning the desk, while she continues to
stare at her screen. She finally finishes, closes her laptop, and
turns her eyes to me, stone-faced; I look at my hands.

"I was just rereading your e-mail," she says. I nod. I wait.
The silence is so heavy. "I wanted to make sure I understood you
correctly. What you're telling me is that your dropping Raejean
onstage was an accident, and that you are quitting the squad. Do
I have all that right?"

"Yeah, that's right."

"And is that all you want to tell me?"

I start a little; Coach just keeps her gaze on me steady. "Um.
What do you mean?" I ask.

"Jenna, sweetheart, you've got no poker face. You know exactly what I mean."

I let out a deep, shuddering breath. "And. I cut Raejean's hair."

"With her consent?"

"No."

"When did you do it?"

"While she was asleep."

"So you committed an act of sabotage against Raejean while she was unconscious."

"Um . . ."

"Yes or no?"

"Yes." I swallow hard and nod and keep looking at my hands.

"Look at me, Jenna." I do. Her mouth is a set, hard line. Her eyes are hard, too. "Sabotaging another team member is at *minimum* a suspension offense."

I've never been suspended before. I just concentrate on holding still under the weight of her words. "Yeah."

"Deliberately damaging Raejean's appearance so that she's no longer uniform with the rest of the team, right before a competition, is a very serious thing."

"I know."

"Do you?"

"Yes."

"So why did you do it?"

I swallow again, but my throat is still dry. "Because I was mad at her."

"Why?"

"Because she's been . . ." I shake my head and look down. "It's a long story. It doesn't matter."

"It absolutely matters. That's why I'm asking you."

"It's just—it's not a good reason. For anything I did. So."

"You're hurt because she hangs out with Meghan now." I look up, and Coach sees the surprise on my face. "Just 'cause I'm old doesn't mean I'm dumb. I can tell when my girls are having a falling-out. You might as well tell me the whole story."

"Um." Deep breath. "She started ignoring me for no reason this year. And, like, cutting me down in front of other people. After . . . I mean, I thought we were best friends. And then for like no reason. No explanation. Just." My eyes are stinging.

"You were heartbroken."

"Yes."

"You still are."

"Yes."

"You feel replaced. Betrayed." I nod. "And, Jenna, I do understand that. I've been there myself. Multiple times."

"Really?"

"Pretty much every girl goes through it at some point." She leans forward and looks hard into my eyes. "But I didn't go and chop someone's hair off."

"No, I know. It was stupid."

"Not just stupid. It was destructive. It was an attack."

"Yeah. I know."

120

"What were you hoping to accomplish?"

"Um. I guess. To make her feel like she made me feel. To stop feeling so . . . stomped on, or something."

"To reclaim your power?"

"Something like that."

"And did you succeed in that? Did you feel like you reclaimed your power?"

"No."

"No. Quite the opposite, in fact, wasn't it? That's why you dropped her."

"It really was an accident, Coach. I never wanted anyone to hurt themselves."

"No, I believe you. I do. But Jenna. I know you did not go out onto that stage feeling powerful and confident. If you had, you wouldn't have dropped your teammate. You see how these two things are connected?" I nod. "You had an accident because you had sabotaged your friend. You did not have an accident out of the blue. You see how your actions have consequences?"

"Yeah."

"All right. So, Jenna." She leans back in her chair. "Your departure from this team would also have consequences. Especially if we are also without Raejean."

I blink. *Wait.*

"Your departure, following this little stunt at competition over the weekend, leaves us without two of our best girls. Is that really how you want to make amends with the team that you just colossally screwed over?"

"Um." I look at my lap again. "I just think it would be better for everyone if I wasn't here."

"Bullshit." It jolts me a little; Coach doesn't swear. "You think it would be better for *you* if you weren't here. Because then you don't have to be reminded every day of your mistake. Because then you don't have to do the hard job of reconciliation and working through an awkward dynamic."

"I really don't think anyone wants to see me right now."

"You think I give a shit?" I blink back the tears in my eyes. "Sometimes that happens on a team, Jenna. Sometimes you do something wrong, *spectacularly* wrong, and piss everyone off. And then you have to keep putting in the work to make it better."

I shake my head, not looking at her, repeating the words I can remember from my e-mail. "I've violated my teammates' trust, and I think my absence will help the squad to heal and move forward."

"Well, I don't. And I am your coach."

The tears in my eyes finally come out at that point, and I try to sniffle them back but end up shaking with silent, full-body convulsive sobs. Coach pushes her box of Kleenex across the desk to me. I blow my nose, but my body doesn't stop shaking. When she speaks again, her voice is quieter and kinder.

"I think the mature thing to do would be to take responsibility for this mistake and work to make it better." I say nothing, shaking and blowing my nose and wiping the rapidly multiplying tears off my cheeks. "It's your choice, in the end. I can't make you stay. All I can tell you is that I want you here." She stands up and walks around to my side of the desk, patting my upper back. "At any rate, you'll be disciplined for your actions. The extent of that discipline is up to Principal Morgan. She'll ask to see you at some point tomorrow."

I can't believe that I'm literally being sent to the principal's office. I've never been sent to the principal's office in my life.

Coach opens her office door for me, and I toss my soggy Kleenex into her trash can, trying to quiet my convulsions. "Let me know tomorrow how you're feeling?"

I nod and leave without looking at her. On my way out, in the parking lot, I see Jodi Lin and Ebony Starker. I don't look at them.

And I know, as I sit in my driver's seat and breathe and blink my way back to composure, that I am not going to come back tomorrow, or ever again.

twenty

PRINCIPAL MORGAN'S PANTSUIT AND LIPSTICK ARE
bright pink. As I tell her, over and over, that I am quitting the team,
the shape of her lipstick mouth slowly changes from a cheery fake
smile to a puzzled scowl. I know, from Coach and my mom, that
the squad is a big deal to Marsen High. Our sports teams may be
garbage, but we have some of the best cheerleaders in the county.
Principal Morgan insinuates over and over that I will suffer fewer
consequences if I stay on the team: "You all are such an asset to the
school, so I'm sure we can work something out . . ." I have to
restate my resignation about four times before she believes me.

"Since you won't need to be at practice, then," she finally
says, "I think a week of detention would be appropriate. And
you'll get an incomplete since this was for phys ed credit—it
won't interfere with your course load since you've already got
two years of it, so you've met the PE requirement, but it will

show up on your transcript . . . really a shame to do this right before college applications . . ." She dials my mother's work number to tell her everything, but Mom's in a meeting, so Principal Morgan tells me that she'll try her again later this afternoon. I think this is supposed to be punishment, too, but I'm just relieved not to be the one to break it to my mom.

My week of after-school detention starts today. I spend the first day sizing up my detention cohorts, kids in dirty sweatshirts or barely there skirts, as I pretend to read *The Great Gatsby*. The detention monitor enforces absolute silence.

When I get home, I see the light on in Mom's room, but I go straight to mine, waiting for her tentative little knock on my door. I wince when it comes.

"Come in."

She sits down so carefully on my bed, where I am lying on my back looking at the ceiling fan, her face lined with worry. A lot happens: She tells me what a mistake this is. She tells me I will regret this. She asks me why I no longer want to get a cheerleading scholarship to college. "Now you'll have to take out loans and be in debt for the rest of your life. Is that what you want?" She had no idea things had gotten this bad with Raejean, and why didn't I say something sooner? "A week of detention? Baby, I don't think you've had detention in your life . . ."

I keep my eyes on the ceiling fan and make sounds when I have to. Yes, no, I don't know.

"I don't think you've thought of this," she says, "but I've sacrificed a lot so you could do cheer."

"I'm sorry," I say.

"Don't you think you and Raejean could talk it out? I just don't understand, all those years of friendship . . ."

I'm not annoyed. I wait for her to run out of questions. But instead, the questions just turn rhetorical and angry: "You cut off her *hair*? Are you a child? What the hell were you thinking?"

I'm grounded for two weeks, which is hilarious, because where would I even go?

Jack's reaction is brief: We pass each other in the kitchen, and he gives me a quick, "You all right?" I nod yes. I have no idea whether I'm lying or not.

When I walk through the halls at school the next day, a couple of kids hiss at me—mostly people I don't know. "Try not to drop me," some football guy yells. But mostly people ignore me. I'm swiftly getting used to being ignored. At detention, the silence alternates between relaxing and oppressive. I have no idea who any of these other kids at detention are.

I decide to eat fast food every day now, since I can. I have nowhere to sit at lunch anymore, so I drive to Wendy's and order off the dollar menu. I last three days before I realize that I don't like Wendy's that much, so at lunch I just go to the parking lot and take a nap in my car. After a week of this, a security guard sees me and tells me I can't do that. I ask him why not, and he tells me to get back on campus. I tell him I'm on the honor roll, I'm not a bad kid, I just needed to take a nap, and he shakes his head and keeps saying "You gotta go back, you gotta go back," over and over. So I go back to campus.

At home, I do nothing. I eat Doritos and do my homework while watching reality TV. Mom makes us eat dinner as a family, and when she asks how my day was, I just say, "Fine." She presses for more info, and I just shrug. My body is screaming at me to stretch it out, go for a run, something, but I don't, and after a couple of weeks my body shuts up.

At Thanksgiving, Mom asks me and Jack what we're thankful for. I say I'm thankful that my body breathes automatically so I don't have to remember to do it.

I have US History with Becca Ruiz. We don't look at each other, and it's fine.

twenty-one

"SO WHAT DO YOU THINK YOU MIGHT WANT TO DO for your birthday?"

It's Sunday, and Mom is sipping delicately on a protein shake, raising her perfectly plucked eyebrows at me in this conspiratorial way that makes my skin crawl. *What kind of naughty shenanigans shall we girls get into?* her face says. It's gross.

My birthday. It's in a week. I'd been trying aggressively not to think about it. How is it December already?

"I don't know," I say, and keep reading the Sunday comics. Garfield is trying to steal Jon's lasagna. In years past, Raejean and I would buy each other enormous balloon arrangements for our birthdays and get them delivered in the middle of class. The cheer girls would all sign a sparkly card for me. Last year, Becca threw me a party at her enormous house and made me Jell-O shots, and I wore a tiara all night.

"We could . . . get manicures. We could . . . go ice skating. We could . . . go see a movie. We could . . . go to the beach if it's warm enough. We could . . . go out for a nice dinner. We could . . ."

"I don't know. I'll think about it," I say, and brush past her to make myself some toast.

She watches me crinkle the bag of bread. "I can make you breakfast," she offers.

"I got it," I say, and don't look at her.

A thing about Mom is she doesn't know when to stop. "Do you want to go to Zumba with me later?"

Her voice is so chipper and so forced that it takes everything inside me not to scream at her. But I don't. "No thank you."

I can hear her pursing her lips without even looking at her. That hurt-feelings, *you don't have to be so obstinate* lip purse. When I was a kid, she'd purse her lips at my dad; now she purses them at me and Jack.

I get the feeling that Mom misses Raejean, too. Raejean and I would always be giggling so hard, and I think that laughter was like a drug for Mom. Before I got my license, the three of us would pile into Mom's car for trips to the mall, all of us talking over one another, Mom begging us to explain some pop song to her. Without Raejean, I must seem like a stranger now. Honestly, I don't recognize me, either.

"So what are you going to do today?" Jesus, her voice gets so high when she gets desperate like this.

"Homework," I say, staring down into the toaster as though that will cook the bread faster.

"Well, it's such a gorgeous day. Maybe you could do your homework in the backyard."

"Maybe."

She shifts so her whole body is facing me. "I talked to Coach Mason, by the way."

I keep staring into the toaster and don't say anything.

"She says that if you would want to return to the team—"

"No."

"Can I finish?"

I shrug, still not looking up.

"She says that she'd be happy to have you back. You and she would just have to have a little chat first so you can talk about making amends to the team, but that you've always been such an asset, and you're welcome back anytime."

"Mom. I'm not going back on the team."

"Well, you can just think about it. Okay?"

I just focus on the toaster, trying to lose myself in the orange-hot grates and the crumbs. Mom stands up, comes to me, and kisses me on the cheek. "You've just been so sad for the past month," she says. "I hate seeing you this way."

"I'm fine."

She smooths my hair, gives me another kiss, and heads to her bedroom. "Just think about it, is all," she calls behind her, and I know that I won't.

My birthday comes the following Saturday. I never did tell Mom what I wanted to do. I don't really want to do anything.

She taps on my bedroom door with the tiniest of knocks, and when I don't answer, she creaks the door open, singing softly. "Happy birthday to you . . . happy birthday to you . . ."

She tiptoes toward my bed holding one of her homemade gluten-free blueberry muffins with a little candle in it. She sits down and holds the muffin toward me, and I blow the candle out.

"There's turkey bacon and eggs in the kitchen," she coos, kissing my forehead.

Hooray. I am seventeen. What a joyful freaking time.

Mom and Jack both got me cards. Mom's has a pastel painting and a poem about special daughters. Jack's just reads *It's your birthday! I got you a card! This is the inside of it!*

Mom went ahead and picked an itinerary for us: manicures and Frappuccinos for "us girls," then a matinee of some chick flick and dinner at Applebee's. I shrug. Sure.

As we're getting ready to leave, the house phone rings, and Jack answers. "Yeah, sure, hold on." He holds it out. "It's Dad."

The Dad phone call—usually stilted, awkward, and short, somewhat like Dad himself—is a strange phenomenon. Sometimes the calls come constantly; my freshman year it seemed like Dad was calling every week or two, asking me and Jack when we were going to come visit him in Colorado, and then disappearing once Mom tried to set plans into motion. Lately, the calls come only on special occasions: Thanksgiving, Christmas, and birthdays. He called one Father's Day to ask why we hadn't called *him*, not believing us when we said we'd been planning to do so later in the day.

I'm not even sure what he does for a living anymore; Jack says he thinks it's something to do with Colorado's weed industry, but it's impossible to figure out for sure. Dad's got a Facebook profile, but he hardly ever posts anything. His much-younger wife, Renee, has an Instagram presence that I'm sure she thinks is inspiring (in which she unironically uses the hashtag #blessed), but he's rarely in the pictures.

I take the phone. My skin feels itchy.

"Hey, champ," he says, like we're old pals.

"Hey."

"How's your birthday?"

"Good. Mom made breakfast."

"Good. Good." There's silence. I'm used to this by now. "How's, uh, how's school?"

"It's good."

"Still making good grades?"

"Yup."

"Good. That's good. I'm proud of you."

You're not.

"And, uh, how's cheer?"

"It's all right. I'm taking a little break from it."

"You are, huh? That's too bad."

"It's all right. It was time." Silence again.

"Well, just wanted to wish you a happy birthday and let you know I love you."

"Thanks."

"Hope it's a good one."

"Yup."

"I'll talk to you soon, okay?"

He always ends the phone call with this, and I used to believe it. Now I just nod, as though he can hear me through the phone.

"Happy birthday."

"Okay. Thanks."

"Bye, kiddo." He hangs up. Our whole phone conversation lasted less than two minutes.

Jack is looking at me from the couch. "Same shit?" I nod. He rolls his eyes. "Asshole."

At the nail salon, I choose deep maroon for my nails, almost black. Mom chatters excitedly to the manicurist about . . . what, exactly? About her friend from Zumba class who has an autistic daughter. About how you can't trust the listed ingredients in food anymore. About how broken our health-care system is. The manicurist just nods, though I think I catch her rolling her eyes at one point.

Over Frappuccinos at a little outdoor table, Mom sighs contentedly and adjusts her sunglasses. "You know," she says. "You may be going through a rough patch right now, but I just hope you don't lose sight of what a remarkable young woman you truly are."

I look at my hands and don't speak, wondering how long this sermon will last.

"You made varsity as a *sophomore*. On a very competitive cheer squad. And even with all the practice and all the meets, you still study hard and get As. I don't know how you do it."

The Frappuccino is giving me a slight brain freeze. I read somewhere that you're supposed to press your tongue to the roof of your mouth to make it go away.

"You're a hard worker, Jenna, and that's gonna take you really far in life. Further than you know. Plenty of people have the talent or the brains, but they just don't apply themselves. And you do. You really do."

The tongue trick worked. I notice there's a bit of dry skin hanging off my bottom lip and I try to bite it off.

"So no matter what, just always remember that your mom believes in you and is so, so proud of you. Okay, kiddo?"

I nod. She puts her arms around me and kisses the top of my head. Then she stares at me, leaning her chin on her hand and shaking her head with this faint little grin, like she just can't believe what a good job she did to create such a magnificent daughter.

I have never felt less magnificent.

The movie is whatever. The white male lead crashes the white female lead's big business conference to effusively declare his love for her because he sees what a fool he's been. None of the actors look like real people to me.

Jack joins us for dinner. He orders a steak. He and Mom chat about drama class and how some of the other techies got in trouble for drinking in the dressing room. I pick at my chicken.

A few classmates I hardly know wish me a happy birthday on Facebook. No one from cheer does.

twenty-two

WINTER BREAK ROLLS AROUND. I SPEND MOST OF
it playing Candy Crush on the couch.

Mom gives me a book for Christmas, something about a young woman overcoming adversity. I don't read it.

Jack and his friends Andraleia and Gemma—oops, James (James, James, *James*)—join me and Mom for New Year's, watching the ball drop on TV and clinking our sparkling cider at midnight. I spend the night concentrating on not screwing up James's pronouns. Mom and Andraleia start an enthusiastic sing-along of "Auld Lang Syne," and the rest of us reluctantly join in.

Back at school, I wander the hallways at lunch with my headphones on, or I sneak out to my car for a nap, lying down in the back seat to avoid the security guard seeing me again.

I spend more and more afternoons on my back in my room, watching my ceiling fan go around and around, pondering how long it's been since I dusted up there. I'm cutting corners on my English and history papers lately, reading summaries online instead of the actual books, but I still keep getting As. Raejean and I used to say, "We're getting a diploma in bullshitting," which honestly seems like the most useful skill we could learn for later in our lives.

Valentine's Day comes and goes. Raejean and I used to make each other over-the-top sparkly valentines, even in high school. This year, Mom just makes burgers in the shape of hearts that night, and the next day she buys a bag of discount sugar-free chocolate for the house.

Two weeks later, I'm staring at my fan, and I can't listen to my thoughts because Jack and his friends are playing their vampire D&D in the living room, and they're too loud. I put on headphones, but I can still hear them, so I march out to the living room to tell them to be quiet.

I'm greeted by a big group "Heeeeeeeeeyyyyyyyyy" that starts with Jack and spreads to James, and soon the whole group is doing it. I stand there awkwardly, shuffling from foot to foot, not wanting to be rude and tell them to shut up now that they've all greeted me in unison. "Hey," I say.

"What's up?" says Jack.

"You guys aren't usually here," I say, because it's all I can think of to say.

"Most Thursdays we do this in the art room," James says. "Today there's an event in there all afternoon, so . . ." He pats the spot on the couch next to him. "Wanna play?"

I don't, but I sit down. I think I see Jack shoot James a dirty look, but James doesn't see; I feel bad for intruding on their game, but now that I've sat down, it would be awkward to get up. "I don't know how."

"Well, first you have to make a character," James says, and hands me a sheet of paper that says *Vampire: The Masquerade* and *Character Worksheet* at the top. "So this right here is your basic character concept, like, I dunno, Child Model or Weapons Dealer or whatever—"

"Child-Model Weapons Dealer!" Karissa with the top hat yells out.

"—and your name," James continues, ignoring Karissa. "And this number here is how many points you get for all these categories—you just have to choose whether you want more points in Physical, Mental, or Social traits. And your Nature is like your essential self, your Demeanor is what you show the world . . ."

"Okay, okay, hold on," I ask. "What does *Clan* mean?"

"Oh!" James shakes his head. "Sorry, of course. So there are seven clans—well, more if you include the Sabbat Clans and Bloodlines, but we're just doing Camarilla so—"

"James, she doesn't know what any of that *means*," sighs Andraleia from the other end of the couch.

"I don't have to play. I don't wanna crash your game." I try to smile.

"You're not crashing. It's not that complicated once you get the hang of it," James continues, undaunted. "So, the Malkavians are insane. Toreadors are artsy. Nosferatu are spies that look like monsters—everyone else looks pretty much humanoid. Brujah are anarchists. Ventrue are snobs. Tremere are sorcerers. And Gangrel are like animalistic nomads."

"Okay. Um."

"Which one do you want your character to be?" James asks.

"I guess . . . artsy."

"Okay, so Toreador." He writes *Toreador* on the Clan line. "What's their art?"

"Um. Ummmmmm. She's a . . ." I almost say *cheerleader*, but that's stupid. How could a vampire be a cheerleader? Cheerleaders kind of have to be awake during the day. "She's a . . . night . . . club . . . dancer."

James pauses with his pen hovering over the sheet. "Like, a burlesque dancer?"

I'm not sure what that is, but I shrug. "Sure? Like in a cabaret."

Axel with the shaved head immediately shouts out: *"Mein Damen und Herren, Mesdames et Messieurs, Ladies and Gentlemen . . . Fräulein Sally Bowles!"* He starts miming an imaginary trombone. James just smiles at me.

"We're doing *Cabaret* next," James says, his eyes wide. "In drama. It's gonna be *lit*."

"Cool," I say.

"You should audition! You can, like, actually dance, from all the cheerleading. They're gonna need dancers."

"Jenna's not a singer, though," Jack pipes up from the corner, and I can't even be offended, because it's true.

"Me neither, but that doesn't keep me from crushing it at karaoke!" says James, bouncing a little bit. "I've got a karaoke machine at home, so you could, like, practice your singing."

"Well, I'm not doing the show, so I don't need to practice," I say, before hastily adding, "but thank you."

"Buuuut, if you did the show, we could hang out at rehearsals and stuff."

I shrug. "We're hanging out now."

He beams at me, then turns back to my character sheet. "Okay, so, we'll put *Burlesque Dancer* under Character Concept—gender?"

"Female."

"Female, Toreador, Burlesque Dancer. What else?"

And I try to think of something else for the character sheet, but I look up and see everyone staring at me, and I suddenly remember that I'm not actually friends with any of these people. I blush and stammer.

"I think . . . um . . . I think maybe I wanna, like . . . think about it?" I take the sheet from James. "I feel like maybe I don't want to come up with all this right now."

"Oh. Okay."

"Yeah. Um. I just need to think about it. Thanks, though." I stand up to go back to my room.

"If you want," Andraleia says, "we're going to a LARP game next Friday night."

"LARP?" I ask. "What's a LARP?"

"It's an acronym," she replies. "Live-Action Role Playing. So, like this, but walking around and actually doing stuff instead of being at a table. On the SDSU campus. It's every other Friday."

"Oh."

"Are you busy?"

No, tiny Morticia, I am never busy. Can't you see that I have no friends?

I always thought the Goth kids were jaded and judgmental. Or maybe they thought I was the judgmental one. At any rate, it's really weird to be invited along. Are they just pitying me?

I don't particularly want to go. Then again, if I stay home for yet another Friday night, I might smother myself with my own pillow. I look at Jack, trying to use my eyes to ask, *Is it cool if I crash your thing?* But he misses all that and just says, "You're not busy, right?"

I meekly shake my head no. James gives Andraleia a smile I can't quite decipher, which she returns, then looks back at me. "Cool. So bring your new character next Friday."

I do my best to smile back. "Cool."

And I disappear to my room.

twenty-three

I'LL HAVE TO FIGURE OUT A WAY BETWEEN NOW
and the game next Friday to tell Jack I'm not going. Today is
Thursday; that gives me a little over a week.

Though, honestly, what if I just went? Could it possibly be
worse than watching my ceiling fan?

I toss aside the character sheet and plug in headphones to
drown out the game in the living room, trying to focus on my
history homework. Mom's got book club tonight, no family dinner, so I gnaw on a Luna bar as I struggle to concentrate.

We're reading about Czarina Catherine the Great, and as
I'm googling, I find out that the *Czarina Catherine* is a boat in
Dracula. I've always liked Czarina as a name.

On a whim, I pick up the character sheet, quickly scrawl
Czarina Catherine under Name, and then set it aside again.

I keep trying to read about Catherine the Great, at least

enough to fake it if I get called on in class. Apparently Czarina Catherine the Great:

- got her husband arrested and deposed and took the throne from him
- made her ex-lover king of Poland
- faced over a dozen uprisings during the course of her reign.

But my eyes keep glazing over.

Raejean and I used to make up characters when we were like nine, acting out the adventures of Lady Whitby and Mrs. Buttress in British accents on the playground. I wonder if this game is like that but for grown-ups.

I pick up the character sheet again. Raejean always fantasized about being a redhead, so Lady Whitby had bright red hair in our imaginations. Maybe Czarina is a redhead, with white skin.

What even is a burlesque dancer? I google it, and suddenly I'm down a YouTube rabbit hole, watching women strip their clothes off as they pretend to be robots and Godzilla and playing cards, or just wearing sparkly lingerie and thigh-highs and making a whole audience scream by taking off an elbow-length glove. Women with names like Dirty Martini and Dita Von Teese and Jo "Boobs" Weldon.

I cannot stop watching. These women are so . . . confident. Wicked. Gorgeous. Like if Heather ever decided to put on a character and strip down to pasties.

What if her whole "act" is being a vampire? So then she can just be herself around the other burlesque dancers, but they assume she's just "staying in character"?

I need to do homework. I set the character sheet down and go back to Czarina Catherine the Great, who never had sex with a horse despite rumors to the contrary. Five minutes later I get another idea and go back to Czarina Catherine, burlesque dancer (what should her burlesque name be? Plasma Junkie? Suck U. Bus?). Then back to history homework, then back to the character sheet.

Was she always a burlesque dancer? Maybe she was a secretary in the thirties, appearing in bawdy variety shows on the side and hoping her boss never found out. Their variety show was one of the best; their reputation was known internationally. Those dancers were athletes, even though everyone always underestimated them.

Maybe she had a falling-out with her best friend at the club where they both danced. Let's give the best friend a name, maybe Mara. Maybe Mara was the flashier dancer, but Czarina was the more solid team player.

Maybe Czarina was turned into a vampire (the proper term for it is *Embraced*, as I find out on Google) by a mysterious older patron of the club, who said she had such a talent that it should be preserved for all time. He checks in on her from time to time. He's fabulously wealthy and helped her out of a financial pickle back in the seventies.

Maybe Czarina couldn't tell Mara she'd been Embraced, and

Mara could tell something was different but Czarina couldn't say what, and they just grew further and further apart. Maybe Czarina is still heartbroken about it.

She misses her mom.

She hasn't been loved in a long time.

I put away my history homework and start typing furiously because there's too much to fit on the character sheet, and googling and typing and googling and typing, and suddenly I realize that I've written seven single-spaced pages of backstory, and it's one a.m. and I need to go to bed.

twenty-four

AROUND THE HOUSE ALL WEEKEND, I KEEP ASKING Jack questions about the LARP game. (It's also apparently just called "game," as in, "Andraleia's giving us a ride to game.") He keeps rolling his eyes at me.

"It's not that complicated," he says. "Basically, whenever there's a conflict, you play rock-paper-scissors to resolve it. Whoever wins gets what they want."

"What if there's a tie?"

"Then whoever has a higher number of traits in that category wins—traits are just, like, points. So, if it's a Social challenge, if you're trying to charm someone into going somewhere with you, then whoever has more Social traits wins."

"But how do you determine how many Social traits you have?"

"I literally just told you this? It's on your character sheet?"

"Oh. Right."

He sighs audibly.

"Do you not want me to go?" I ask.

"No, you should go."

"I won't go if you don't want me to go."

"Do you even want to go?"

I shrug. "Sure."

"So go."

"Okay." I think for a second. "Should we make it so my character already knows your guys' characters?"

"Well, if they don't know each other, then that would give her a reason for being a fish out of water, you know?"

"Sure." So we decide not to tell each other about our characters.

———————

Two days after that conversation, in the living room after dinner, I tell Jack, "I'm worried that I'm gonna say something stupid to James."

"Stupid like what?"

"I don't know. I just don't know anyone else who's transgender."

"You literally just treat him like a person. It's not that complicated."

"Okay. Sure."

"Literally you can just google this stuff."

"You're overusing the word *literally*."

"I'm using it accurately. You are *literally* able to go on your phone and just look it up."

"What do I even look up?"

"I dunno, 'shit not to say to transgender people'?"

So I do, and I read on my phone as Jack reads Anne Rice.

"What's hormone therapy?" I ask Jack.

"Like taking testosterone so your voice changes and you grow body hair and stuff. Or estrogen, for trans women."

"Has James done that?"

"Not that it's any of your business, but no, his mom's making him wait until he's eighteen. So that part's mostly gonna happen when he's away at college."

"Oh. Is his mom not cool with him being trans?"

"Nah, she's basically supportive. She bought him his binder."

"What's a binder?" I ask. "Like a notebook?"

"It's this thing you wear that makes your chest flat."

"Like a sports bra?"

He sighs, loud. "Can you just google stuff so I can read in peace?"

"You could just go to your room."

"I was here first."

We sit in silence for a while; I'm the one to break it.

"Thanks for letting me crash your thing."

He shrugs. "Sure."

I offer to drive us to game, but apparently Andraleia takes everyone in her mom's minivan. "It's tradition," Jack says. I try to put together an outfit befitting a burlesque goddess, but the closest I can find is a lacy lavender tank top, which I wear with a tight pair of pale blue jeans. Jack wrinkles his nose at my outfit, his eyes ringed with thick black liquid eyeliner, and says, "You're going to wear that?"

"Why not?"

"You'll just stick out."

"Does everyone dress super Goth?"

"Yeah, I mean, it's vampires."

"But isn't that the most obvious choice? Like, wouldn't you wear regular clothes if you were a vampire so no one would suspect you?"

He just shakes his head. "Do whatever you want."

Mom kisses us both on the cheek on our way out the door. "So glad you two are doing this together! Be safe! Love you!"

We're the last ones to get picked up, so Jack and I have to get in the very back. I sit in the middle, between James and Jack. Andraleia yells out our last name as we squeeze in: "Heyyyyy, Watsonnnnnsssss!" Everyone in the car is wearing black. Black denim, black vests, black pleather pants, black crushed velvet. Andraleia's dress has big black bell sleeves that dangle out the window as she smokes a clove cigarette.

"I dig your character choice," James shouts over the loud, screamy music that Andraleia is cranking.

"What?" I shout back.

He shouts louder: "The pastels! So she can blend in to regular society! It's so smart!"

"Thank you!"

Everyone but me headbangs to music that I have never heard

before. Axel tries to steal Karissa's top hat, but she steals it back, and they kiss.

"You nervous?" shouts James.

"Kinda."

"It's easy once you get the hang of it. You can ask me questions if you get stuck."

"Okay. Thanks."

Game is played outdoors on the SDSU campus, where the players gather in a big courtyard. I watch as all the people who know each other hug, air-kiss, high-five, say hi. Everyone, with the exception of a splash of red or deep purple here or there, is wearing black.

I hang back until a towering Asian woman who must be in her twenties, with bloodred lipstick and a black shiny corset, approaches me and gasps, one hand to her chest and the other gesturing at me. "What is this? Fresh meat?"

"My little sister," Jack says. I sigh. *Can you not call me that?*

"Oh my goodness! Baby Watson is coming to join us!" She gives my outfit a once-over and puts both hands over her heart. "So innocent! A springtime maiden! Look at you!" I just make myself smile. "My name is Gracie," she says, "and I'll be your host this evening."

"Gracie's the storyteller," James tells me. "What she says goes."

"And you are just so yummy and pretty, I could just eat you up! May I kiss your hand, darling?" I nod. She takes my hand and plants a red lipstick kiss on it; I notice Korean characters tattooed on her fingers. "Welcome . . . to Plagues of the Night."

Gracie is so tall I have to tilt my head back to make eye contact. "Hi." She continues to hold my hand in hers.

"Now, did Jack explain the rules to you, Baby Watson?"

"Yup."

"And you understand that once game play begins, you are to remain in character at all times?"

"Okay. Sure."

"And what is your character's name and clan?"

"Czarina. She's a Toreador."

"Wonderful. Oh, it's so lovely to have new blood, darling. Pun very much intended. Thank you for joining us." And then she's off to greet new folks in a twirling whoosh of black skirts and stiletto boots and woodsy-smelling perfume.

James, smiling, nudges my arm. "Don't worry," he says. "I won't start calling you Baby Watson."

"You better not." I motion toward Gracie. "Is she always so . . ."

"Intense?"

"Sure."

"Generally, yeah. She's great, though. Just overwhelming when you first meet her." Two pasty guys in glasses greet James, and he introduces me to them: Roger and Carter. I shake their hands and pretend not to notice them looking with confusion at my clothes.

Once everyone has arrived, we all huddle together (maybe two dozen of us) as Gracie stands on a bench in front of us. "Good evening, Kindred!

"Welcome to Plagues of the Night! Tonight . . . everything is different. And yet everything is the same. Mayor Madeline Rocher is still missing, and the city is still searching for her high and low. But tonight, when you woke up, you felt something . . . different.

"Malkavians, my lovely loonies: Whatever your insanity, tonight, when you woke up, you simply . . . didn't have it. Tonight, mysteriously, you are all, suddenly, sane."

Players throughout the crowd grumble and mutter and shout "What?!" including Jack and James. But Gracie just holds up her hand, and everyone almost immediately quiets down.

"Toreadors: Tonight, you woke up without your artistic talent. Whatever your gift—painting, dancing, exceptionally well-planned murders—you find yourself suddenly unable to do it."

The hubbub of the crowd bubbles up again. I do quick calculations in my head. *Okay, so, Czarina can't do burlesque. How can she not know how to strip? Is she just suddenly very clumsy about it?*

Gracie keeps addressing different clans while I think: *Okay, so she's probably got a show tonight, maybe she can call out sick, maybe she can get a friend to help . . .*

"You have all received a mysterious message tonight. Those of you with electronic devices may have received it via e-mail or a text message from an unknown number. The elders among you who may eschew such things have received a paper note. Whatever the medium, the message simply contains an unfamiliar address, followed by the word *midnight*. There is no signature.

"It is now ten p.m. Your character has two hours to rearrange their plans for the night and see if they can find out any gossip about what this mysterious message might be regarding. Good luck."

Everyone breaks into smaller groups and starts talking among themselves. I tap Jack's arm. "Now what?"

He blinks at me. "Just do what Gracie said."

"But my character doesn't know any of your characters."

"So we'll make them meet."

"But . . ." He's moved his attention to James and Andraleia. Andraleia has adopted a little-girl voice, and James keeps tenting his fingers like a bad guy from a movie.

"Mr. Biggles," Andraleia says in her little-girl voice, "I feel so different. Why do I feel so different?"

"I know not, my child," James says in a deep British accent.

"Like everything was so spinny spinny WOOOOO before, and now it's just, like, *normal* and *boring*. Do you feel like that, too?"

"Yes, my child."

"And what's this stupid meeting at midnight tonight? I wanna stay here and watch cartoons!"

Slowly I piece the story together: Andraleia's character (Janie) was turned into a vampire as a child; James (Mr. Billingston, but Janie can't pronounce that so she calls him Mr. Biggles) is her sire, the one who turned her. Jack enters the scene, cowering like he's got a humpback: "Master, what can I do for you?" Apparently Jack (Matthew) is a mortal that Mr. Billingston feeds vampire blood to, which gives him superpowers but also makes him kind of Mr. Billingston's slave—they call him a ghoul. Karissa and Axel play a brother and sister, Mr. Billingston's archenemies, who are in incestuous love with each other. "Our love can never be consummated," Karissa sighs, "for sexual things no longer bring us pleasure since the Embrace."

It's cheesy, but I can't stop watching them. Like a soap opera with vampires.

I watch them for about ten minutes, until Andraleia's character exits the scene and quietly comes over to me, speaking in her normal voice. "So. What's your character's deal?"

"Oh. Um . . ." I start in on the backstory about doing variety shows in the thirties, but she stops me.

"No, but what's she doing *now*?"

"She's a burlesque dancer. Her whole shtick is that she's 'pretending' to be a vampire onstage but she's, like, actually a vampire."

"But like right now. What is she doing right now?"

"She's . . . heading to the burlesque venue. She's . . . I guess she's trying to figure out how to get around the whole not-being-able-to-do-art thing, and get out of the nightclub before the midnight meeting . . . ?"

She skips back into the scene as Janie. "Mr. Biggles, I changed my mind! I wanna go see ladies dance before our dumb, boring midnight meeting!"

So they change the setting to the burlesque venue (how they got a child into a nightclub is not discussed), where Janie wanders up to me in the dressing room. "Hello, stripper lady!"

I look to Jack. "How did she get in here?"

"Because she's three and a half feet tall," Jack says. "No one noticed."

"Okay. Cool." I try to put on Czarina's voice: older, confident, a bit of a diva. "Oh, child, where did you come from? This dressing room is no place for a small girl." And then I find that James has snuck up behind me, and I jump. "Oh my God," I laugh. "You scared me." Suddenly my eyes lock with Gracie's; I don't know when she got there or how long she's been watching our scene.

"*Character*, Baby Watson," she says, wagging her finger.

"Right, sorry." And I try to go back to the scene.

"How did you two get in here?" I gasp, trying to sound indignant. "This is a private area!"

Jack pipes up from the sidelines. "She's right. Billingston, you need to throw chops to use Obfuscate."

I blink. "What?"

"We need to play rock-paper-scissors to see if I can sneak into your dressing room," James says. So we throw chops, and James's scissors beats my paper. He gets into my dressing room unobstructed.

"My, my, my," James purrs from behind me, "what have we here? You've got that bloodsucking act, don't you?"

"That's right. I'm Plasma Junkie, and the blood of my prey is what keeps me alive," I say as Czarina. I try to kind of purr the words.

"It's a pleasure. I'm Mr. Billingston."

"Mr. Biggles!" Andraleia yelps.

"Ms. 'Junkie,'" James intones, "may I ask whether you received a mysterious message tonight regarding a certain midnight meeting?"

"Wait, did you send that?"

"Oh, no, my dear. I only wished to determine whether your act was just that—an act—or whether my hunch was confirmed: You are, indeed, one of the Kindred of America's Finest City. So pleased to have you among our company."

I try to smirk. "Charmed, I'm sure." I look up to see if Gracie is satisfied with my character work, but she's gone on to observe another group. James pats my shoulder and whispers, "Don't worry. You're doing great."

I try to channel Gracie as I pretend to powder my nose: "Darling, I'm just having the strangest night. I feel like I couldn't shimmy to save my life." I implore their help with my burlesque act, and we have to throw chops to see if they agree to my plan, but my rock beats James's scissors, so I win. We figure out a solution together: Little Janie (who's really several decades old, but never lost her childlike ways) will join me onstage and pour buckets of stage blood on me. That way I don't actually have to dance, since I woke up without my "powers," but the audience still gets a show, and then we can go to the big meeting together.

When all the vampires gather at "midnight" in game time, we are treated to the big reveal: Mayor Madeline Rocher (played by Gracie) has been Embraced by Prince Alan Hannibal (I guess a prince is like the mayor of vampires), played by a towering guy in a white suit who looks familiar for some reason. Prince Hannibal proudly shows off his new progeny, and they both make speeches about helping to make San Diego a safer city for the Kindred.

Some of the clans are not pleased about this news, and someone tries to attack Mayor Rocher. A vampire riot breaks out, and Jack has to walk me through the process of navigating fights via rock-paper-scissors; I lose most of my turns, so Czarina gets punched in the face and trampled underfoot (which, fortunately, no one is allowed to actually act out, only narrate), but she stays alive.

As the riot reaches a fever pitch, Gracie shouts out: "Toreadors! Your talents suddenly mysteriously return, and you feel compelled to all express them at once! Malkavians! Your maladies all suddenly come back, and you feel compelled to all express them at once!" So suddenly the crowd is full of howling and muttering Malkavians and Toreador singers singing or actors reciting Shakespeare, and amid the chaos I decide to go ahead and do Plasma Junkie's burlesque routine, and I mime taking off a glove, a feather boa . . .

By the time game is over, I finally feel like I'm ready to start playing.

twenty-five

THERE'S AN AFTER-PARTY. IT'S A BONFIRE ON THE beach, where all the Goths roll their black jeans up and wade into the Pacific Ocean. A couple of them go skinny dipping, though the water must be freezing. It's significantly more low-key than the cheer parties, for which I find myself grateful.

I sit in a vacant camping chair and stare into the fire, glad to have somewhere to put my eyes. I feel wired and exhausted all at the same time. James plops down on the sand next to me.

"So how was your first experience with game?" he asks.

"It was . . . good!" I say. "Yeah, good. There's just so many rules and stuff."

"Yeah, that happens," he says. "I know it's a lot to learn, but it's worth it to keep at it. Game is my favorite thing."

"Why?"

"Because you can be whatever you want! Do whatever you

want! We get to be immortal for a couple hours. I mean, that's pretty awesome, right?"

I smile. "I've always thought living forever would kind of suck," I say.

"Well in *reality*, sure, but you get to decide what things are like for your character, so you can decide that immortality would be totally amazing." He looks away from the fire to look at me. "I'm selling you on it. I can tell."

"A little bit," I admit. "I'll give it another shot."

"Oh man, that's so great!" He looks back to the fire. "Plus vampires are just hot."

"But like . . . vampires can't really have sex, right? Like Karissa and Axel?"

He shrugs. "Only if your definition of *sex* is totally heterosexist."

"Sorry. I didn't mean—"

"It's fine." He cuts me off. "I just mean—so, yes, vampires can quote-unquote have sex, but they just don't get a lot out of it anymore. Feeding on blood is the closest thing they can experience to the feeling that sex used to give 'em—but if something's bringing you that kind of ecstatic pleasure, then I kinda think, like, that *is* sex! So if you think that sex equals what we were taught about in health class, then yeah, that's not how vampires get their rocks off, but like—there's so many ways to experience pleasure, right? I just think the definition of sex should be broader than rubbing junk together."

"That's fair," I say. I'm not positive I agree, but I'm not sure I disagree, either.

He looks back over at me. "You're queer, right?"

I stare back at him, confused. "Did someone tell you I was?"

He starts stuttering. "Oh, I—I just thought—didn't you punch some guy a couple years ago for harassing you and your girlfriend?"

It takes me a second to realize what he's talking about; then I feel my face fall, and I can tell James sees it, too. "No," I say. "That wasn't me, it was the other girl, and she wasn't my girl-friend; she was just my—friend. My ex–best friend. We were just . . . holding hands."

"Oh." There's silence, and it's a little awkward, but it's also okay, because there's a fire, and we can both look at it. "Man," he says, "I really remembered that story all wrong."

"It's all right," I say.

"I just thought it was super cool that you were a cheerleader and you were queer. Like that movie, *But I'm a Cheerleader*. Have you seen that?"

I laugh. "Yeah," I say, "I didn't realize what it was when we decided to watch it, though." That had been some freshman-year movie night with Raejean, giggling through all the sexual parts because we didn't know what else to do. We were so immature back then.

"So you're straight?"

"I . . ." I don't know how to answer. I think about the imagined threesome from sophomore year with Raejean and Mikey Wall and the millions of nights cuddling with her in my bed, and I don't know what category to put any of it under. I finally say, "I've only ever gone out with guys."

He nods, almost to himself, and then he stands up. "Well, that's fine," he says. "Because I'm a guy. And I think you're super cute. And I'm gonna go get a soda now." And then he just walks away.

I stare after him. Did he just say what I thought he said?

I can tell I'm blushing, or maybe it's just the fire, and I'm glad that it's so dark. I stare into the flames, trying to process what I just heard, and a million feelings I never considered having about James suddenly hit me at once. Okay, James thinks I'm cute. Do I think he's cute? Does "I think you're super cute" mean "Let's do something about this," or is it just a statement of fact?

There's really only been one significant guy in my dating life. For the month of April of my sophomore year, Roland Jackson and I called each other every night. We made out on couches at Becca Ruiz's parties and in his back seat down the street from my house before he dropped me off. He had red hair and high cheekbones and gave me my first (and only) non-self-induced orgasm with his fingers. I didn't know him that well, but I knew he was the junior-year class president and smelled like a magazine cologne sample. Our phone calls were largely silence, in between questions like "What's your favorite color?" and whispering what we wanted to do to each other's bodies.

I started feeling guilty when I was hanging out with him; he'd be trying to start some stilted conversation, and I'd just want him to shut up and make out with me. I was worried that if we kept at it, I'd lose my virginity to him, and the thought of having that first experience with someone I found so profoundly boring kept me up at night. So I dumped him. In retrospect, the whole "relationship" was an exercise in feeling like an adult, in proving to myself that I could do this, see someone every week and touch each other and even enjoy it. I would recount every detail to Raejean, who was hooking up with Ben Park the soccer player, and we analyzed every moment like sports announcers. What we liked and didn't like. What we thought they might do next time. What we wanted that they hadn't done.

Still, I feel woefully unprepared for the great unanswered question at the end of "I think you're super cute." Roland had taken care of all the questions for me by asking Raejean for my number, texting me **Hey whats up its Roland how r u** and kissing me at Becca's party. The ball had never been in my court until I dumped him.

But right now in front of the fire, I can tell that the ball is very much in my court.

Tiny Andraleia totters across the sand in her enormous black platform heels, throwing more firewood on the fire with a clove cigarette hanging from her mouth. I point at her shoes. "Don't those hurt?"

She shrugs. "Nah, I'm so used to them by now. I wear heels more often than not 'cause I'm so short, so . . ."

"Right."

"You did good tonight. For your first time."

"Thanks, I feel like I had no idea what I was doing."

"Nah. You were fine." She drags on the clove cigarette. "My first time at game, I didn't realize how much of it was, like, physical fights?"

"Wait, but not literally, right?"

"Oh, no, it's just the characters who're fighting, *we're* not fighting. We're just playing rock-paper-scissors. You're actually literally not allowed to touch people without asking," Andraleia says.

"Gotcha," I reply, and then I remember Gracie asking before she kissed my hand. I look down at the lipstick kiss. "I think that's a good rule."

"Right? So I created this character with all these really high Social attributes and really low Physical attributes, and then we ended up in this big vampire brawl and I just got, like, *clobbered*."

"Yeah, I got kinda clobbered tonight."

"I know—it's kinda demoralizing. But you get over it."

We look at the fire together, and I marvel at the diffusing power of the bonfire, how magically comfortable and easy silence can be as long as there's a fire there. I point to her clove cigarette. "That smells nice."

"You want one?"

"No, I'm good."

"You want a drag?"

". . . Okay." I shouldn't, but screw it, I don't have to keep myself healthy for cheer anymore, so why not?

She hands it to me gingerly. "Careful, it's stronger than a regular cigarette. Tastes better, though." I take what I think is going to be a small drag, but she's right—it's strong. I manage not to cough and hand it back to her.

"It does taste good," I say.

"Yeah. If you lick your lips, they taste like clove."

I try it and laugh. "Yeah, they do."

I take a great big breath of bonfire-ocean air and feel my shoulders drop down. Jesus, what is this? Am I . . . relaxing? I don't know if I've relaxed since I left the team. I take another big breath, feeling even more tension leave my shoulders. I can't remember the last time . . .

"Jenna! Hey, Jenna!" My brother is calling to me from across the fire. "You did a number to this, right?"

I don't know what he's talking about at first, but then I listen and realize there's been music playing this whole time, pumping out of tinny iPhone speakers on top of the cooler. And in the same breath I realize that the song playing is the one we used for Heather's homecoming routine.

"You did a cheer routine to this?" asks Andraleia, and James starts chanting, "Do it! Do it!" and then they're all chanting it. I stand up almost without thinking, not even because I want to, but because I want them to stop chanting.

"It's gonna be harder to do it on the sand," I try to say, but they keep chanting: "Do it! Do it!"

So I do.

Handstand. Legs bent like I'm riding a bike. Switch switch switch switch switch switch switch HOLD, switch switch switch switch switch switch switch HOLD, then skip-saunter into what

164

would be the formation if there were anyone else doing this with me . . .

I loved this routine so much. It was sexy and energizing. Right now it feels like lifting a heavy box or something.

And fast: arms high V, then daggers, then hands to your forehead while you pop your ass back, right leg over left, turn all the way around and smack those hips, snake your head right, straight, right elbow and left knee to the chest, step down, arms in a pike and hips go right, left, right, clasp, center splits to the floor, onto your tummy . . .

And now I'm lying in the sand and I don't wanna get up and I hear myself say, "I think I'm just gonna stop here, guys."

There's scattered applause and *awww*s. I don't look at anyone. And I realize that the reason I stopped was because the next move in that routine was the lift I did with Evelyn Rice, and as much as I never want to see Evelyn again, I stopped because I loved doing that lift too much to mime it.

I fold my arms under my head and close my eyes. The sand feels nice and cool, especially with the warmth of the fire on my face, but I feel like I'm going to cry, and I don't want to do it in front of strangers. So I get up. "Gonna take a walk," I say, probably too quiet for anyone to hear, and I walk down to the water's edge.

They're those annoying not-quite-tears, the ones that insist on staying in your face and making you feel like you're going to hyperventilate without actually letting you have any release. I speed walk along the water's edge, trying to move fast enough to get the tears flowing, but they just bunch up and sting my eyes.

"Hey! HEY!"

I turn around, and James is running to catch up with me. "Jesus, woman, you move fast," he pants.

I stop walking. "Sorry."

"No, no—" He stops with his hands on his knees and tries to catch his breath. "I'm, uh." Deep breaths. "I'm sorry we made you dance."

The tears finally decide to come out. "Oh no," James says. "I've said the wrong thing."

"No, you didn't. It's okay." I don't want to cry in front of him, but it appears that I don't have a choice.

"You okay? Scratch that. You're not okay. Um." He stands there, and I can tell he doesn't know what to do.

And I tell him everything. Raejean falling out of friend love with me, and Meghan, and homecoming, and cutting her hair off, and quitting the team in disgrace. I tell him all of it, with snot running over my upper lip from the crying, and he quietly hands me white fast-food napkins from his pocket, which I use to blow my nose, and I keep talking until I've told him the whole story. And I don't have pockets, so he just takes my snot-filled napkins out of my hands and bunches them back into his pocket, and I can't tell if it's gross or sweet, but I think it's sweet.

"I'm sorry," he says.

"Thanks."

"My best friend divorced me, too. When I came out. She said she didn't believe me, said I just needed to learn how to feel more comfortable being a butch woman, and it turned into this really stupid political thing, and . . . we don't talk anymore."

"I'm sorry that happened," I say.

"I'm not," he replies. "She sucked."

"Yeah, sounds like it."

He looks at me for a really long moment, and just the pro-longed eye contact starts making me blush, but I don't think he notices. "Do you want a hug?"

I nod.

We hug for a really long time. My insides flutter and flutter and don't stop. I bury my face in his shoulder and breathe deeply. "You smell so good," I say.

He laughs. "Enjoy it now," he says. "It's gonna go away when I start testosterone, 'cause that shit makes you smell *horrifying*."

I laugh. "I didn't know that."

"Yeah, it's a whole second puberty. Like the first time wasn't bad enough."

We're still hugging. It's been over a minute now.

"Am I gonna kiss you?" he asks, and I laugh. "Guess not." His voice sounds defeated.

"No, I just mean"—I consider breaking the hug to look him in the eye, but decide not to—"it's just funny how you worded that. Not like 'Is it okay if I kiss you?' or 'Should I kiss you?' but 'Am I gonna kiss you?' like I'm Miss Cleo or something; it's just . . . funny."

He's quiet. But we're still hugging. "I don't think I'm gonna kiss you right now," he finally says.

"Okay."

"I don't mind if you kiss me, but I think I'm not gonna make the first move tonight."

"I don't think I'm gonna kiss you right now, either," I say.

He finally breaks the hug and looks at me. "But maybe some other time?"

"Well," I say, "I don't really know you." And he looks at the ground. "But . . . I'd like to? Know you?"

He looks up and nods. "Okay. I can work with that."

And then we're just standing there, staring at each other next to the ocean.

"Are you sure we're not gonna kiss each other right now?" he asks.

"Um . . ." I think about it. Part of me definitely wants to. Part of me is thinking about my brother and all his friends sitting back by the fire, wondering if they're watching us. James sees me hesitate and nods.

"Okay, that's a no," he says. "Can I kiss you on the cheek, though?"

"Okay."

And he does, so softly, and I can feel myself blushing again, and I start giggling, and I look at him to make sure he knows I'm not giggling in a bad way, and he starts giggling, too, and I grab his hand for just a second, and then we walk back to the fire in silence, the kind of silence that's gentle and not oppressive, and I don't think I've felt this good since the school year started.

twenty-six

JAMES STARTS TO SEND ME PLAYLISTS.

The first one comes at three a.m., after the bonfire, while I'm asleep. I sleep through the notification, but in the morning I see James's note: **Just some songs I wanted to share with you.**

Most of them I've never heard of. A lot of them are loud. A lot of them are about a girl: Bikini Kill's "Rebel Girl," the Dresden Dolls' "Girl Anachronism," Peaches's "Boys Wanna Be Her," Janelle Monáe's "Q.U.E.E.N." The overtly sexual ones, like Nine Inch Nails' "Closer," he includes with a disclaimer: **Not trying to drop any hints, it's just such a good song.** Some love songs: Joanna Newsom's "Does Not Suffice," Metallica and the San Francisco Symphony playing "Nothing Else Matters" live. Some political: Rage Against the Machine's "Killing in the Name," a couple of Kendrick Lamar tracks. And then some are just weird:

El Perro Del Mar's "God Knows (You Gotta Give to Get)" and early Regina Spektor B sides.

I don't like all of it. But I listen to it from beginning to end, lying still and flat on my bed with my headphones on, and some of the songs make my stomach feel tight inside. When I listen to it a second time, I find I like some of the songs more than I thought I did. I text him and tell him my favorites.

He writes back: **Do you want me to send you more? I have so much music.**

Then without waiting for my response: **Am I coming on too strong? I just really like sharing things I like.**

I write back: **Yes to the first question, no to the second.**

James: **:-)**

It occurs to me that if I started dating him, some of the girls on the cheer squad might call me a dyke. Which is so stupid, because, hello, Coach Mason is married to a woman. Then I remember that I hate them all and don't care.

For the next four days, James and I don't see each other at school, but he sends me two more playlists. He builds them around themes: "Rainy Day, or Staying In Just Because," and "Songs to Make You Feel Amazing." I look up the artists I like and download their albums. I start to put my favorites into a playlist of their own. We keep texting, mostly about the music and what we're doing that day.

Mom keeps coming in my room without knocking, ugh.

I'm so hungry but too lazy to get up.

Hope you're having a good night.

On Thursday, as I do the wander-around-campus-at-lunch thing, I pass by their posse: Jack and James and Andraleia and Karissa and Axel. James tries to wave me over, and I just wave back, not wanting to intrude. So he walks over to me. "I just downloaded some St. Vincent," he says. "Do you like her?"

"I don't know," I say. So he grabs my hand and pulls me over to the table where they're all eating lunch, and we share a pair of earbuds. He plays me three songs—wobbly symphonies of distortion.

"What do you think?"

"I love it," I say, and then the bell rings.

"I'll send it to you," he says as we pack up our things.

"Okay!" I say, and I can't stop smiling.

After school that day, I see James and Jack talking in hushed voices in the parking lot as I walk out to my car. I wave at them as I walk, but James runs after me again.

"Hey!" he says.

"Hey." I suddenly feel shy around him. "What's up?"

"Nothing. What're you doing?"

"Nothing. Going home."

"Cool. You, uh." He looks at his feet. "You wanna hang out, or . . . ?"

". . . Yeah! Yeah, um, I mean I've got homework and stuff, but I can do it later, so . . ."

"Cool! Okay. Let me just—one second." He runs back to Jack at the other end of the parking lot, says something to him, and then runs back to me. "Okay, let's go."

"What was that about?"

"Nothing."

"Were you getting my brother's permission to hang out with me?"

"No! It's like literally nothing." I can see that he's blushing, and then I realize: Today is Thursday—the day they play their tabletop game. James is skipping out on their game to hang out with me.

"Let's just go," he says.

"Where are we going?" I ask.

"Um. I dunno. Do you like ice cream?"

We sit in my car in the 31 Flavors parking lot with our cones for about three hours, running inside for seconds at some point and bringing them back out to the car again. We talk about being raised by single moms and major illnesses we had as kids (pneumonia for me, tonsillitis for James). We talk about vampires and movies that scare us and how neither of us has ever had pets. We talk about being bad at kickball and how traumatizing that is in fifth grade. We talk about our favorite cartoons and both being forced to do ballet as children, which turns into a running joke in the conversation: "Plee-aaaay aaaand straaaaight! Plee-aaaay aaaand straaaaight!"

We don't talk about me quitting cheer or his transition, and that feels nice.

It's really easy to talk to him.

My face hurts from laughing.

When I drop him off, there's another lingering hug like the one on the beach. It lasts a few minutes. We just don't let go.

"What are you doing Saturday night?" he asks.

"I'm never doing anything," I say.

"Can we go on a date? Like a movie? Can we call it a 'date'?"

"Okay."

"You sure?"

"Yeah, I'm sure."

"Cool."

We finally pull apart from the hug. The will-we-or-won't-we again of whether to kiss or not. We lean our foreheads together while we decide. Finally he just rubs his nose against mine. "Bunny kiss," he says, and I laugh. He gets out of my car, and once he's inside, we just keep staring at each other and making faces through his living room window, until finally he waves goodbye and disappears from view.

twenty-seven

I CHANGE MY OUTFIT FOR OUR DATE NO FEWER
than seven times that Saturday, eventually settling on a form-fitting
flannel shirt that I hope makes me look down-to-earth yet cute,
with denim shorts and chunky red heels. Mom takes it upon herself to hover in the hallway and ask about my plans; I lie and say
that I'm hanging out with Alison Boyer from English class. She
squeals with joy at the news that I'm leaving the house for once.

When I pick James up at his house, he's wearing a black vest
and black jeans, and I find myself checking out his butt when he
turns around to lock his front door behind him. We get Olive
Garden in the big mall complex before our movie, gorging ourselves on unlimited breadsticks and soup and salad, making up
imaginary characters named after different kinds of food, like
Fatty Prosciutto and Cherry Tomato. "So they're a crime-fighting
duo," James says.

"Totally. Cherry Tomato has to be a redhead lady, and Fatty Prosciutto is a big Italian guy."

"Right! He used to be in the mob, but now he's one of the good guys." He puts on a fake Italian accent: "Heeeeey, it's Fatty Prosciutto!"

The movie is funny and gross. It's got a bunch of *SNL* actresses in it. I laugh, but James laughs harder. He laughs so hard he grabs my arm as though he has to steady himself.

When the movie gets serious and the heroine has to apologize to her best friend for screwing things up so bad, James puts his head on my shoulder and lets the back of his hand rest against the back of mine. I move my hand into his, and we interlace fingers. A big Italian-looking guy comes on-screen, and I murmur, "Heeeey, it's Fatty Prosciutto!"

When we get into the car afterward, we just stare at each other. "I don't wanna go home," he says.

"I don't, either."

He finally leans across the radio and the stick shift and kisses me, hard and soft at the same time, and I kiss him back, putting my hand behind his head. Then he pulls back. I can feel myself blushing, probably all over my body, can feel my pulse banging on my skin, and I wonder if he can see it in my throat.

"Was that okay?" he asks.

"Yeah."

"I haven't kissed anyone in a while, so you're the first person I've kissed who knew that I was . . . me. So I just wanna make sure it's okay."

"Yeah. It's okay."

"Can I kiss you again?"

"Yeah."

He kisses me again, a little softer this time, and the tip of his tongue just barely brushes mine. I pull him as close to me as I can manage in the car. We push our tongues farther into each other's mouths. He digs his nails into my lower back through my shirt, and I gasp. "Sorry," he whispers.

"Don't be sorry," I say. "It felt nice." And I keep kissing him.

After a few minutes, he stops and asks, "Do you wanna go somewhere?"

"Like where?"

"Um. I think the parking lot behind the bowling alley is generally pretty empty . . . ? Don't ask me how I know that."

I laugh. I try to think fast. I want to keep doing this, but I don't want to keep doing this in the car.

"If you come over," I say, "my mom won't think anything of it 'cause she'll think you're there to see Jack. If she even sees you."

"Okay. Cool."

I drive us home, go in first, and tell him to count to 100. Mom is on the couch with her friend Zoe from book club; they've got cocktail glasses in hand and are giggling incessantly. "Hi, honey." Mom beams, and I kiss her on the cheek. "You have a good night?"

"Yup! Hi, Zoe!" Mom's about to ask me more questions, but I practically run into my room. "I'm exhausted! See you in the morning! Love you!"

I wonder whether to turn the lights out, or to change my clothes or something. I don't do anything. I just sit on my bed paralyzed, listening to the hum of Mom and Zoe's chatter, and thinking that James must be counting very slowly.

Finally I hear the front door. "Oh, hello, James!"

"Hey, Mrs. Watson." I can hear the nerves in his voice, can hear him trying to play it cool, and I hope my mom doesn't hear what I'm hearing.

"Zoe, this is Jack's friend James." I hear the murmur of introductions. "Jack's just back there," Mom adds, and I know she must be pointing down the hallway, where Jack's room sits across from mine.

"Cool, cool. I'm just gonna, uh, use your bathroom real quick."

"Oh, go right ahead! It's just right there . . ." I hear the bathroom door open and close, and then silence except for Zoe's laughter.

Please, Mom, don't watch him come out of the bathroom and come into my room. Please keep paying attention to Zoe.

More silence. Running water. More silence. What is he *doing* in there? I crack my door as quietly as I can and peek down the hall. Zoe's the one with the perfect view of my room, but Mom's back is to me. They don't notice me. Everything holds still.

Then the bathroom door swings open, and James and I are staring at each other through the crack in my door. I look at Zoe; Zoe doesn't see me. I motion James to come in. He rushes into my room, and we slam the door and kiss each other. Without taking my mouth off his, I lock the door behind us.

I try to sit us down on the bed, and he stops, standing with his eyes on the floor. "I don't really know what I'm comfortable with," he blurts out.

"What do you mean?"

"Like I just . . . have no idea what's okay with me? I don't think I'm gonna know until we're like . . . just, if you start doing something and I tell you to stop, it's nothing personal. Or like maybe we should just ask each other before we do anything."

"Okay. We can do that."

"Cool. Um." He takes a deep breath and sits down. "So kissing's okay."

"Okay." And we do, for a long time, sitting on the edge of my bed.

"Is it okay if we lie down?" he finally asks.

"Yes."

We lie back and keep kissing, ungracefully kicking our shoes off as we do. I feel his fingers against the skin of my lower back.

"Can I put my hand up the back of your shirt?" he asks.

"Yes."

He does. His fingers slip under my bra strap but don't unhook it yet. He runs his short fingernails over my back, and I shiver.

I move my hand from the back of his head around to his collarbone. "Is it okay if I unbutton your shirt?" I ask.

He stops moving and thinks about it. He takes a deep breath. "Okay, but leave the undershirt on," he says.

"Okay." I keep kissing him while I undo the buttons, while

I slip the sleeves off his shoulders, leaving his black cotton tank top with the binder underneath.

We keep going. "Can I undo your bra?" "Yes." (So he does, and before he can ask if it's okay to move his hands onto my breasts I tell him he can do that, too, and he does, and he doesn't squeeze them hard like Roland Jackson did; he just holds them gently.) "Can I straddle you?" "No, sorry." "It's okay." (So I don't, and we just keep pressing our bodies against each other, hard.) "Can I bite you here?" "Just don't leave a mark." (And he bites my neck so softly that I get chills all over my body.) "Can I move my hand down?" "Not tonight." "Can I pull your hair?" "Can I kiss you here?" "Can I take this off?" "Can I—"

We stop sometime around one a.m., panting and giggling, arms and legs and torsos all flung together. He kisses my neck. "I'm glad we did this," he murmurs.

"Me too."

I look up at the ceiling with a huge smile on my face and breathe deeply.

The light is still on.

twenty-eight

ON SUNDAY WE TEXT EACH OTHER ALL DAY.

I can still smell you.

I feel like I'm high.

Having trouble concentrating on anything.

I listen to his playlists on repeat and stare at the ceiling. I clutch a teddy bear and barely leave my room. I have to masturbate to get to sleep.

Maybe our LARP characters could have an affair. Maybe Czarina seduces Mr. Billingston. That would be so hot.

On Monday I text him before school: **Your "Songs to Make You Feel Amazing" playlist works even on Mondays :-)**

He doesn't respond. I consider finding him at lunch but decide not to.

After school I text him again: **How were classes?** No response.

I spend my whole night trying to read my calculus textbook and failing. *It's probably fine. He's probably just busy. I probably shouldn't have texted him so much yesterday. Maybe he just needs space. I can do space. It's fine. Maybe I should just say hi. Nope, not gonna do that.*

All day Tuesday I check my phone obsessively, sure that I must have missed a text from him. I am determined not to text him again. Then I do: **Miss me?**

He responds immediately: **Yes.**

I send him a smiley. No response.

How's your week going? No response.

Sorry. You're probably busy. I'll stop bugging you. No response.

WTF DID I DO WTF DID I DO WTF DID I DO? I listen to the most heartachy songs on his playlists and replay every moment of Saturday night, looking for something I might have done wrong, some moment when I might have done something he wasn't okay with, and I can't find a single thing.

Radio silence on Wednesday. I manage not to text him, mostly by turning my phone all the way off.

On Thursday I have the thought that if I find him before their tabletop game after school, he has to talk to me. I try to pretend the thought never occurred to me. Then my feet walk themselves over to the classroom where they have their game, and I stand there and wait outside. Jack's other friends say hi to me as they go in. Andraleia waves excitedly and beams: "Are you joining us today?!" I shake my head no and try to smile, my voice caught in my throat. Jack gives me a weird look on his way in but doesn't say anything.

James is the last one there. He avoids my eyes as he approaches. "Hey," he says to the floor.

"Hi," I say. I have no idea what else to say. "What's up?"

"Not much," he says, still not meeting my gaze. "Sorry I've been bad about . . ."

"No, no, it's fine," I hear myself saying, and it's not fine, but I can almost, in this moment, convince myself that it's fine.

"I gotta . . ." He trails off and points in the direction of the classroom.

"Can we just . . . ?" I have no idea how to talk right now. "Um. Just. Are we gonna go out again, or . . . ?"

He finally looks up at me and sighs. "This is probably a longer conversation than we have time for right now," he says.

"Okay."

"Just . . . I missed last week, so . . . I should probably go in."

"Sure." I look at the floor. I feel like I'm exploding.

He comes close to me, grabs my hands, and kisses them. "I had a really wonderful time with you. Okay?"

I look into his eyes and nod. I can't talk. I don't know what's happening.

He goes into the classroom. I go home.

I know I shouldn't, but I immediately start texting him again: **Did I do something wrong?**

And: **Please just lmk if I did anything that wasn't okay, I would hate to have messed up without knowing it**

And: I really like you a lot

And: Sorry if this is too much I just am kind of confused

And: When can we talk?

And: Trying not to come on too strong but I just wanna know what's up?

And: If you just don't like texting that much that's totally fine, I just thought you did

And: Sry if I'm overreacting

And on. And on. I can't stop myself. Why can't I stop myself?

Finally at 9:13 p.m. he responds: Can you come over?

I'm over there by 9:25. He comes out from the house and sits in my passenger seat. We don't look at each other for a long moment.

"Okay," he says. "I really, really like you."

"I like you, too," I reply.

"More than I realized I was going to." I don't respond to this because I can't tell whether that was a compliment or an insult. He finally looks over at me. "You know I'm going away in the fall, right?"

I just look at my lap. *Right. College. Duh.* How did I forget that James was a senior?

"And. I'm gonna start T over the summer. And things are just changing really fast for me, and I just think maybe . . . maybe right now isn't the best time for me to . . . I know if we keep this up that I'm gonna fall for you. More than I already have. And. I don't think it makes sense, right now, to throw a relationship into the mix . . ." He takes a deep breath. "I didn't mean to lead you on. I just . . . didn't know."

There's a silence that feels like forever. Finally I say, "Didn't know what?"

"That I would feel this way about you. And, like, the full implications of that."

"So what did you think was going to happen?" He looks down and doesn't answer. "No, seriously. That's not a rhetorical question."

"I don't know what I thought was going to happen."

"Well, do you think you might wanna put a little more thought into that next time?" I can feel myself losing control. "Like, did you think I was just someone to hook up with?"

"No! I just didn't know, okay?"

"You just did a total one-eighty on me. You were acting *so* into me, and then you just blow me off?" I say, and I hate how accusatory I sound, but I'm *right*, damn it; I know I'm right. "Why?"

He sighs. "I just . . . learned some things that made me see things differently."

I shift in my seat. "Learned things about me?"

"No. I—so I'm on this Reddit forum for trans guys. And I went on there, and I was gushing about you, and everyone was super happy for me and supportive and stuff, but a couple guys were just like, 'Okay, but how's it gonna feel if she, like, breaks up with you in the middle of you transitioning?' And sharing their stories, like coming back from college with their deep voices and their girlfriends being all like, 'I feel like I don't even know you anymore, this is too hard for me,' and they were just like, 'Are you willing to risk that, like, in the middle of already being in an unfamiliar environment at college and everything?' And I just decided . . . I'm not."

My stomach drops. "So we're stopping before we even start because strangers on the Internet said so?"

"No," he says. "This is one hundred percent my decision. It's just a more informed one now."

"I don't care that you're going away," I practically yell. "I think it's stupid not to give this a shot just because you're afraid of me dumping you. That's so dumb."

"You say that now," he says quietly, "but my body and my voice are gonna change while I'm away, and I'm gonna come back, and you're not gonna recognize me—I don't know what's gonna happen to *me*, okay? I might be a total wreck about the whole thing; that's not fair to you."

"So I could be there for you!"

"No, you couldn't," he says, "because you'd still be here."

Something breaks in my chest.

I start hitting my steering wheel over and over and hyperventilating. James reaches over to put his hand on my arm, to stop me, but I don't stop. "I'm sorry," he says.

"Do you even know the kind of year I've had?!" I reply, and I am full-on screaming by now. "Do you have any idea how shitty everything has been?!"

"Yeah, I do," he says, and he's so calm it makes me ashamed, but I can't stop.

"You knew what kind of shithole I was coming out of. You *knew* that. And then you pull this shit?! Why did you even talk to me?!"

He tries to rub my back, but I jerk away from his hand. "You're taking this really hard," he says.

"Seriously?"

"Just . . . we went on one date, and . . ."

"Okay, well, why did we even go on any dates?! Why did you even ask me out? *You* pursued *me*, remember?"

"I know."

"I just really didn't need this right now. Like, why didn't you think of all this before you asked me out?"

"Because I didn't know."

I rest my head on my steering wheel, willing myself to breathe slower, to stop talking and stop making everything worse. We sit there in the quiet for a while. "I've just had such a shit year," I finally say again.

"I mean, mine hasn't been all that great, either . . ."

"It seriously doesn't need to be a competition, James."

Our eyes meet, and I can tell he feels bad about all this, but he seems annoyed with me, too. I look away first. "Weird question, but . . . did you ever get closure with Raejean?" he asks. I shake my head no. "Well . . ." He looks at his lap again. "Maybe this isn't totally about me?"

I sit up and look at him. "What?"

"Like. Maybe you're actually upset about Raejean. Not me."

I press my face into my hands and shake my head. "No, no, no, that is not what's happening."

"Okay. Never mind."

"I LIKE YOU! I WAS FALLING FOR YOU! THIS HAS NOTHING TO DO WITH RAEJEAN!"

"Okay, okay . . ."

"I mean, is there something wrong with me?! Is there a freaking *sign* on my back that says 'Abandon Me'? Like WHAT IS ACTUALLY HAPPENING HERE?"

"I mean. Sometimes stuff isn't about you, you know?"

"What does that mean?!"

"Well, I can't speak for Raejean. But for me, this decision has nothing to do with you, and everything to do with my life circumstances. It's not personal. Okay?"

I try to take deep breaths. When I talk again, my voice is much smaller. "When is it ever gonna be about me?"

He smiles at me, and I can see how this is a smile I could keep looking at, a smile to greet me after class every day, the smile he would give me right before kissing me, and my heart breaks because I'm never going to get to live that out.

"I'm sorry," he says again. "In another life . . ."

He grabs my hand with both of his and kisses it, over and over. I close my eyes and try to stop time.

Then he gets out of my car and goes back inside, and I hit my steering wheel over and over and cry until I am howling, and I can't stop.

twenty-nine

I GO HOME, AND I LIE ON MY BED WITH MY SHOES on and this feeling like a million bricks are stacked on my chest. I don't know how I'll ever get up again.

When I was in the car, I wanted to punch through walls. I wanted to scream and cry until it ripped my body apart. Now I just want to stay here and let the world cave in on me.

I was so close.

For a second, it had seemed like I might actually survive the school year. Like I might live through everything. Like I might even, occasionally, have fun and be around people I like. Like losing Raejean and leaving cheer wasn't a death sentence.

And now that's all gone. Now I can't see James again and I can't go to game again and I can't hang out with any of Jack's friends again and I guess I'm just going to be alone forever. Great. Just great.

There's a knock on my door. I ignore it. My lights are on, but maybe Mom will still think I'm asleep.

"Jenna?" I hear Jack's voice from outside my door. "Can I come in?"

I decide to ignore him.

"Jenna?" The door cracks, and I bolt upright.

"Why would you open the door without me saying you can open it?!" I yell.

"Sorry," he says, "just didn't know if you had headphones on."

I sigh. "Come in."

Jack comes in and sits at the foot of my bed, looking down at my feet. "Why are your shoes on?"

"Because I haven't taken them off yet."

He looks at me with this kinda soft look I'm not used to seeing from him. "Do you need a hug?"

No, screw you, I don't need your pity. But I nod. I do need a hug.

He puts his arms around me, and I bury my face in his sweatshirt, trying to block the whole world out. "James told you?"

"Yeah."

"Why?"

"Because he feels bad."

"He should feel bad."

"I know."

I feel like crying, but I don't. I break the hug and cover my face with my hands. "I just feel really stupid."

"Why?"

"Because we literally only went on one date."

"Really? It was just the one?"

"Yeah."

"Because he talked about it like it was this bigger thing. He talked about it like a relationship."

"Ugghhhhhh, don't *tell* me that!"

"I just thought you should know he didn't take the decision lightly. If that's any comfort to you at all."

". . . Thanks." It's not, but it is at the same time. I flop back on my bed and stare at the ceiling.

"Did I ever tell you about me and Andraleia?" Jack asks. I shake my head no. "Well, last year, I decided I was totally in love with her and that we should be together and I had to tell her that."

I lift my head to look at him. "Really?"

"Yup."

"What'd she say?"

He laughs. "She said thanks but no thanks."

I laugh, too. "Did she break your heart?"

"Into a million pieces."

"Man, that sucks."

"And nothing ever even happened there! It wasn't like we had something and then it got taken away from me. It was literally all in my head. But I still was just, like, I couldn't sleep or eat or do homework. I felt like there was no reason to be alive or do anything."

My stomach drops a little bit as I realize that that's why Jack's grades had slipped from As to Bs last year, and that I hadn't even noticed he was in pain; I'd been so deep into cheer and Raejean and whatever else I was doing, and meanwhile my brother had been going through hell right under my nose. "But you guys are friends now."

"Yeah."

"How did you do that?"

"We took a little space from each other, and then . . . tried hanging out."

"Just like that?"

"No, I mean, it took time. But she still cared about me, even though she didn't want to be my girlfriend. And I'd rather have her in my life than not have her in my life, so . . . we figured it out."

"Are you still in love with her?"

"Nah. I mean, I don't know how much of that is sour grapes and how much is just time and getting to know her better, but there's certain ways in which I think she would drive me nuts if she was my girlfriend."

I keep staring at my ceiling, following the blades of the ceiling fan around and around and around. "I don't know if I want to be friends with James," I say.

"You don't have to."

"I mean I might. I don't know. I kind of hate him right now."

"Don't hate him. He's trying."

"I'm allowed to hate him if I wanna hate him."

"Okay. Hate him. Just, like, stop hating him at some point. Hate is really time-consuming."

I roll my eyes. "What are you, a therapist?"

"I mean, I wanna be."

"Really?"

"Well, that's the plan. We'll see if any colleges actually let me in."

"I didn't know that."

"There's a lot you don't know." He stands up. "You good? You need anything?"

"Nah. I think I just need to listen to a shitload of sad music and curl up in a fetal position."

"K. If you need something, you know where I live."

"Thanks."

"Yup." He leaves and closes the door behind him.

The amount of bricks stacked on my chest has shrunk from a million to maybe a few thousand.

Slowly, I take my shoes off and tuck them under the bed.

Thirty

THE NEXT DAY I PAY ATTENTION IN ALL MY CLASSES.
I raise my hand and ask questions. I don't actually care about AP
Biology, but it's something to do. Something to think about that
isn't James.

At lunch I walk the campus in circles, always pretending I'm
on my way somewhere. Just keep moving.

While I'm circling, Jack texts me: **Do u wanna keep doing
LARP?**

I write back: **Probly not. Don't wanna see J.**

A few minutes pass, and then: **He's willing to switch off w/u
if u wanna keep going.**

I stop and stare at my phone. I laugh. Is this dude serious?

I write back: **Like shared custody? LOL**

Jack replies: **Basically**

I think about it. Game is tonight. Do I want to see all these people who know what happened, who probably take James's side, who barely know me?

Then again, do I want to stay home forever?

I think about my character. Czarina. I think about her burlesque act, all her fellow performers so confused because she never seems to age a day. I think about her bloodred hair and her wealthy sire and her preternatural, diva-level confidence.

I like Czarina. I like *being* Czarina.

I text Jack back: **Sure. He can take tonight.** I can stay home and keep working on Czarina.

"You're not going with your brother?" my mom asks that night, head cocked to the side.

"No," I say. "I'll go next time." Jack has just left without me; I'm in pink sweatpants and a messy bun, trying to escape this conversation.

"You all right?"

"Yeah, just felt like staying in."

Mom stares at me with one of those mother-knows-best little smirks, a smile that says, *You know I don't believe you, so we might as well drop the charade right now.* I try to ignore her and go to my room.

"Why don't you sit down with me," she says, sitting down on the sofa and patting the spot next to her. I sigh as audibly as I can and flop down.

"What?"

"What's really going on with you, honey?"

I cover my face with my hands. "Oh my God, *Mom*."

"No, I'm serious. You quit cheer, then you try going to your brother's game, and then you quit that, too. You huff and flounce around this house and don't talk to me. Why don't you want to do anything?"

"Because everyone is an asshole! Raejean decided all of a sudden this year to be a complete jerk to me—actually so did the entire cheer squad—and then one of Jack's friends turns out to be a total piece of shit, so . . ."

"Honey, if everyone's an asshole, maybe the asshole is you."

"I *am* an asshole. But also, maybe high school just sucks."

My mom rubs my arm, and I resist the urge to jerk away from her touch. "Which one of Jack's friends was mean to my little girl?"

"Um. James."

My mother raises her eyebrows. "James? James was a piece of . . . crap to you?"

I look at my lap and nod. Please don't make me go into detail, Mom. Please just let me go to my room.

"What did he do?"

I shake my head. "I don't wanna talk about it."

"You never wanna talk about anything, sweetie. Nothing's gonna get better if you never talk about it."

I heave the biggest sigh I can manage. "Fine! He pursued me and asked me out and waited until I was getting attached to tell me he's going through too much right now and can't actually date me. Okay?!"

My mother turns her body to face me fully. "You and James dated?"

"One date. He broke it off last night."

"I wish you'd tell me when you've got someone romantic in the picture."

"Why? So you can hover and embarrass me?"

"So I can be part of your life! Jesus, honey, I wanna know when something's making you happy or making you sad! I wanna know your life!"

"You mean, live vicariously through me?"

She bites her lip, and her face distorts, the way it would back when she and Dad used to fight all the time. "Do you honest to God think you're the only person in this house with feelings?"

My jaw drops, and I don't respond.

"You don't talk to me; you don't say thank you; you give me attitude when I dare to ask how you're doing, like it's this huge imposition! Like I'm such a jerk for having the nerve to care about your life! Maybe sometimes you could try being grateful that your annoying mother is looking out for you. Maybe sometimes you should just shut your damn mouth."

I feel my whole face puffing up, and I put my hands over my eyes, but Mom keeps talking.

"You and I used to be such pals," she says. "What happened?"

I start to cry into my hands.

"No, that's not a rhetorical question," she says. "What happened? What changed to make you treat me this way?"

"I've just had such a hard year," I say through my tears.

"Well, just 'cause life is hard doesn't mean you get to treat people like garbage. Especially when those people are working their fingers to the bone to keep you from starving or living on the street."

I wipe my eyes, my stomach still heaving with sobs. "So, what? You want a gold medal for feeding your children? You want an award for not starving me? Congratulations! You're mother of the year!"

"Oh Jesus Christ, Jenna. Do you have any idea how spoiled you are? Do you even know how hard I hustle to take care of you and your brother?"

"We all know you work hard, Mom. You love reminding us of it so much."

"Will you shut up? Will you just shut up for one second?" We stare at each other with our tear-streaked faces, hyperventilating and puffy eyed. She takes several deep, slow breaths, and when she speaks, her voice is calmer. "You know why Jack doesn't give you grief for driving the car more than he does?"

I blink, surprised. This is not at all the question I expected. "Because he doesn't need it as much as I do?"

"Because I told him not to. Because if I'm not driving you around to cheer practice and competitions, I can do more overtime at work. Baby, I don't even *remember* the last time I put in less than fifty hours at the office. I do *everything* for you."

I grab some Kleenex off the coffee table and blow my nose. "I thought you liked your job."

"I like my job just fine. Doesn't mean I wouldn't rather be

home with you and your brother. You two are my whole world."
She waits for me to respond, but I can't think of anything to say
to that, so I just look away. "You should just think a little more
about how you're affecting the people around you is all. You
should just think a little more about that." She keeps taking deep
breaths, her face slowly returning to its normal color. "I'm sorry
that I yelled at you."

I roll my eyes. "Sure you are."

"You are not an asshole, Jenna. You are a remarkable young
woman who happens to sometimes treat the people who love her
like trash." We sit in silence for a long moment, and as much as
her words feel like getting stabbed in the stomach, I can't help
thinking that she's right.

"I'm sorry," I say.

"I'm sorry, too." She stands up and wordlessly goes to the
kitchen, coming back with two glasses of water. She hands me
one, and I gulp it down. "And," she says, "I'm sorry that James
hurt you."

"Thanks."

"You deserve to be treated well."

"Thank you."

We sit in silence for a while. "I'm still gonna go to game,"
I say eventually. "Just not tonight. Me and James are gonna . . .
switch off."

"Good!" she says, finally cracking a smile, maybe a little too
forcefully. "Do you like the rest of Jack's friends?"

"Sure. They're nice."

"Yeah, I think they're nice, too." She sips her water, her eyes far away. "I also wouldn't take it too hard, if I were you. James's life is full of a *lot* of changes right now."

"I know. Everyone keeps telling me that." She puts her hand down and takes mine. We hold hands in silence for a while.

"You think you might ever wanna go back to cheerleading?" she asks.

"Nah. I'm done with that."

"You really loved it."

"I did. But that's over."

"I'm sure that if you and Raejean talked it over, you could work it out."

"I don't think so, Mom."

She tucks my hair behind my ear. "Well. I know I'm not perfect, either. But I love you more than anything. And you can always talk to me about anything at all. Okay?"

I nod. "Okay. I love you, too."

"Oh, good."

We sit in the quiet for a long time, holding hands.

thirty-one

MOM MAKES WAFFLES THE NEXT MORNING, AND I
drill Jack about what happened at game. "What's the deal with
the mayor? Tell me everything."

He laughs at me. "Apparently she's told the city council that
she has a very rare illness that requires her to only meet at night.
Allergy or something. So she's keeping up appearances."

"Okay—but why did we all change last time? The Malkavians and the Toreadors? Why'd we all lose our madnesses and
talents at the same time?"

"That was some Tremere shit. They've been clashing with
both clans a lot lately."

"Tremeres are the sorcerers?"

"Yep, that's right. Look at you."

My mom sets down the plate of waffles with a smile on her
face. "I thought you'd only been the one time!"

I shrug. "Just trying to keep on top of things."

"Gracie asked about you," Jack says. "She told me I had to bring you back."

"Really?!"

"Why, honey," my mom says to me, "you're beaming! I might even call that a shit-eating grin!"

Jack wrinkles his nose. "How come you get to swear and we don't?"

"Because I'm the mommy, that's why."

For the next week, in between analyzing *The Fountainhead* for AP English, I continue writing Czarina's backstory. I want to immerse myself in Czarina. I want to imagine myself so deeply inside Czarina's head that I can forget that Raejean and James don't love me.

I write the scene where she gets Embraced and becomes a vampire:

"You wanted to see me, Dr. Müller?"

"Why, yes, child, come in. Why don't you take off that lovely scarf of yours."

After her Embrace, she knows she has to keep the secret from Mara, and this pushes them apart—forcefully, painfully. *"I just don't understand—it feels like you're miles away from me all of a sudden . . ."* And in the end, Czarina is the one who has to end the friendship, for Mara's sake. She leaves her a letter when she quits the variety show: *Please know that you have meant the entire world to me, but all good things must come to an end.*

I create a timeline of all the events between when she gets Embraced and the present:

- She was engaged to a sweet guy in the fifties, a mortal, but then Dr. Müller found out and got terribly jealous, so that was the end of poor Jonathan.
- She fronted a punk-rock band in the eighties and even had her own groupie "ghoul" for a while, to whom she fed her own blood in exchange for unquestioning loyalty. (He died in a bar fight.)
- She enjoyed some financial success in the early days of the Internet; she could pass as an eccentric entrepreneur who would only work at night. Her company, WorldToday, was a primitive website that would aggregate news from different websites into one place; one article called her "enigmatic web mogul Czarina Catherine . . ." She sold her company in just the nick of time before the dot-com bubble burst.

After a week of this, I assemble everything into one master document and bounce out of my room to find Jack and tell him everything I've figured out about Czarina.

He's in the kitchen with Mom, both of them hugging each other and squealing. "I can't believe it! Oh, honey, I can't believe it!"

Jack got into his first-choice college. It's in Michigan.

thirty-two

MY MOM IS BOUNCING AROUND THE KITCHEN AND
screaming. "Holy crap holy crap holy crap!" She keeps looking at
the acceptance letter, jumping up and down, hugging Jack, and
then starting the whole cycle over again. "Jack! Honey! This is
huge!" He just smiles, looking down at the floor and blushing
that trademark Watson blush. "And they're offering so much
financial *aid*! Holy crap holy crap!"

I stand in the doorway of the kitchen and just watch them.
My mom yells at me, "Honey! Give your brother a hug! He got
into the University of Michigan!"

I do.

She stands with the letter in one hand and her other hand
over her mouth, tears flowing down her cheeks. "My baby's
going to be a shrink," she says quietly. "Why are they letting
babies become therapists? You're my baby. I gave *birth* to you."

"I'm a legal adult, Mom," he mumbles, but he can't stop smiling, either.

"I'm taking us all out for ice cream. We need to celebrate this."

She disappears to her room to change. "You're leaving me," I say. I try to make it sound like a joke, but it doesn't come out like a joke.

"I'll be back," he says. "For holidays and stuff."

"Yeah, but you won't *be* here."

"Nope. I won't."

I think about our conversation in my room, about how hard it was for him after Andraleia rejected him, how I'd had no idea he'd been hurting, and I realize I will never get that time back.

So I just stick my tongue out at him. "*Michigan*," I say with as much disdain as I can muster. "You know Michigan's freaking cold, right?"

"Don't miss me too much," he says. "You'll be fine."

"Who said I was going to miss you at all?"

"Yeah, okay." He does an impression of me in a high, girly voice. "'You're leaving me! But it's chill; I'm totally not gonna miss you.'"

I try to give him a noogie, something I haven't done to anyone since probably fifth grade, but he ducks away. His eyes land on the letter again. "Can I see it?" I ask. He hands it to me. The letterhead feels so stiff and official in my hands. My eyes glaze over, and I look away.

"Your first-choice school," I say.

"Yup."

"Why Ann Arbor? Seems kinda random."

"Well, it's apparently the fourth best college in the country for psych majors, even though you can get in with less than a four point oh, which is good 'cause I've got some Bs. But then I kept finding out more about them, and I just . . . really wanted to be there."

"You're gonna freeze your balls off."

"Yeah, I know."

"Seriously, though," I say, trying to pack my words with sincerity, "congrats. That's a big deal."

He nods. "I know. Thanks."

"Are you so happy?"

"I'm really happy, yeah."

"Good. You deserve to be happy."

"Thank you. You do, too."

thirty-three

CAN I BORROW UR CLOTHES TONIGHT? IT'S JENNA BTW

It's game night again. Jack gave me Andraleia's number. I stare at my phone, text sent. Was it weird to ask that?

She writes back: **Sure, what's ur size?**

At my house that night, she gives me an expert smoky eye, and I wiggle into my fishnets from my middle school talent show. "Decided not to go the pastels route tonight?" she asks.

"Just trying something different." I consider rambling about how my outfit last time made me feel too cutesy, and I want Czarina to feel powerful, and also I don't like sticking out so much, but I stop myself before I start.

Andraleia holds up a dress. "So, this is a little longer on me than I want it to be, but I'm super short, so it might be just right on you. What do you think?"

I pull it on. It's a stretchy black pencil dress with a lace inset around the waist. Something Czarina could throw on after performing. The hem hits me just a couple of inches above my knees. "It's perfect," I say.

"Keep it," she says. "I never wear it."

She brought bloodred hair extensions, which I clip into my brown hair. "You told me Czarina was a redhead, so . . ."

"No, this is exactly right. This is great." I look at myself in the mirror, then at Andraleia. "Do I look okay?"

"You look friggin *hot*."

I've been googling Vampire: The Masquerade rules all week, watching tutorials online. "Is it gonna be a problem not having James there? Since Mr. Billingston is your sire?"

"Nah, we figured it out. We invented all this business that Mr. Billingston has to attend to in Japan, and while he was gone, *my* character, little Janie, started having Jack's character, Matthew, do *her* bidding, which is hilarious 'cause she's like seven. It's bloody amazing. Pun intended."

"Does anyone know Mr. Billingston's first name?" I ask.

Andraleia laughs. "Nope."

In the van on the way to game I recognize a song from one of James's playlists. "Is this Bright Eyes?"

"Sure is!"

"Turn it up?"

At game, Gracie as Mayor Madeline Rocher pulls Czarina into a new mission. "Prince Hannibal and I do not see eye to eye on our vision for this city," she says. "I wish him no harm, but he needs to be stopped." We have to kidnap the prince—the familiar-looking super-tall guy in the white suit. Gracie fixes me with her eyes. "Are you up to the challenge, Czarina?"

I stand up tall. "Count me in."

The physical challenge to get the prince out of the bar and into our limo falls on me and five other players I don't know. Each of us throws chops to try to subdue him, but somehow the prince player keeps winning every single game of rock-paper-scissors. We are all trying to stay in character, but I can see a couple of people starting to choke back laughter as we lose round after round.

Then I look up from our hands for just a moment, and I see a small pale girl standing behind the prince. My jaw drops. Hers drops, too.

"Heather?!"

"Jenna?!"

Instinctively, though we have never ever done this before, we dash to each other and hug. She's wearing a black spaghetti-strap dress that laces up the front like a corset, with black tights and combat boots. She fits right in here. You'd never guess where we knew each other from. And that's when it hits me why I felt like I'd seen the building-tall guy before: Adam, her boyfriend, from church. The giant I met at homecoming. No wonder he looks so familiar.

"What are you doing here?" I gush.

"Me? What about *you?*" she lilts in her Polish-accented voice, and I can't believe I never noticed how charming she sounds. She giggles as she holds me by the forearms, looking at my borrowed clothes, my attempt to fit in. "You stop cheerleading so you can pretend to be a vampire?"

"My brother brought me," I explain, pointing him out. He's currently ensconced in some kind of group rumble a dozen yards off or so. Heather looks at Jack and turns back to me with an open-mouthed smile.

"How have I never met your brother! This is so wild."

"Ladies. *Character.*" Adam's booming voice sounds like being admonished by the bowels of the earth itself, but Heather just laughs and puts her arms around his waist.

"Character? All right, my love. *Natasha* intercepts and— Jenna, who is your character?"

"Czarina."

"Takes Czarina to the corner of the bar for a little chat. Someone else must get the prince into the limousine." She grabs my arm and walks me over to a concrete bench a little ways away from the action. The bench is cool on the backs of my legs. "Natasha and Czarina," she laughs as we sit. "Couple of Russian broads. Who'd have thought?"

I smile. "It's good to see you," I say.

"It is *so* good to see you, Jenna! I did not think our paths would ever cross again."

"I . . ." I don't want to ask the question, but I can't not. "I thought you would all hate me. Doesn't everyone on the squad hate me?"

Heather shrugs. "Yes and no. Coach did not inform us of your reasons, so we were left to draw our own conclusions.

Raejean has still been present, something like an assistant coach while her ankle was healing. But she does not talk about you. There are some who think you dropped her on purpose, but they are the minority. I never thought that you did."

"Did she tell you guys I cut her hair?"

"But of course you did."

"She told you?"

"No, she does not talk about you, but it is the only explanation. Nobody gets a haircut in the morning before a competition. Especially nobody as vain as Raejean is." I laugh, and Heather smiles back. "I must say, to cut off your friend's hair, that is a crazy thing to do. I was surprised because you always seem like a very level-headed person."

She says it without judgment in her voice, but I look away. "I'm really not. I'm kind of a crazy person."

She grabs my arm suddenly. "I just remembered how you were screaming outside on the night of the homecoming dance. You *are* a crazy person."

"Yeah, I am." We both laugh. I didn't realize I would be so happy to see her. "How are things on the team?"

"Oh, you know." She shrugs. "Not our best year. We did not make it to State." Wow. Our first time in ten years not getting to State. I feel a pang of guilt, remembering my conversation with Coach. "I am just glad I got to choreograph the homecoming routine. I was very proud of that."

"Heather, I still do that routine in my mind while I'm trying to fall asleep. I *love* that routine. It's one of my favorites."

She beams at me. "Thank you for saying that. I hope that the next coach will continue the tradition of letting a student choreograph the homecoming."

"What next coach?"

"Next year. After Coach leaves."

"Wait, what?"

She fixes me with a long gaze. "You did not know?"

"Coach is leaving?"

"Her wife's mother has been diagnosed with Alzheimer's, so they are moving to the Bay Area to be close to her. Coach has already found another position, in Berkeley."

"Wow." I feel myself blushing, as though this is all my fault somehow, even though that's ludicrous. "Who's replacing her?"

"They don't know yet. They had just better not be terrible."

"I mean, no one could ever replace Coach."

"That is so true. We are doing a big tribute to Coach at the end of the year."

"Really? Wow."

"Pieces of her routines from over the years. Some alumni are coming back to participate. I am so surprised that some of these women from ten years ago still have their uniforms." She turns to look at me. "Would you want to participate?"

"Oh . . . no, I don't think so."

"Why not?"

"I wouldn't want to ruin the day for anybody."

"But Coach told us she invited you to stay on the team. I think she would be happy to see you."

"I just . . . don't think I belong there anymore."

She shrugs. "Well. You will let me know if you change your mind?"

"I will."

We watch the other gamers in the distance. Someone is spinning around and around in the middle of a circle for some reason. "Probably we should go back," Heather says.

"Yeah, probably."

"Wait, what does Czarina do?"

"Um. Burlesque dancer?"

"An artist! Are you a Toreador?"

"I am, actually."

"Me too. Natasha is an assassin. That is her art."

"Uh-oh. Am I her next mark?"

"You had better hope not."

And we rejoin the group. And Natasha ends up enlisting Czarina's help, using her as a spy so she can get to the guy she's supposed to kill. And Czarina doesn't realize at first that she's being used as a spy, but once she figures it out, she decides to keep helping because she likes Natasha. And when the time comes to kill the guy (Jack's character, Matthew), he wins rock-paper-scissors and narrowly escapes with his life, but realizes he has to stay in hiding now and figure out a plan to kill Natasha before she kills him. And Natasha goes home to her eight-foot-tall lover and employer, and Czarina goes back to performing.

When game is over for the night, we go to the bonfire on the beach, where Heather and I re-create old routines on the sand,

and she giggles all through the story of how she met Adam, and Axel has a flask and I take a sip, and Gracie tells me I did an amazing job tonight and we plant lipstick kisses on each other's cheeks.

And when Heather and Adam run off to take a walk along the water and make out, I lie down on my back in the sand, and I see how many stars I can count, and when Jack sees me lying down and asks if I'm okay, I tell him, "Yeah, I'm good." And he lies down in the sand next to me and we look at the stars and don't say anything.

thirty-four

ON THE WAY HOME, ANDRALEIA ASKS IF ANY OF us want to go see a movie with her tomorrow, a new horror movie that's just come out, something with chain saws. No one is free. She looks at me in the rearview mirror. "What about you, Jenna?"

"What about me?"

"Are you free tomorrow?"

"Oh—oh, yeah, I totally am, I just didn't know you were asking me, too."

"Why would I not be asking you?"

I just smile and shrug. "Yeah, I'm free."

She picks me up in the minivan the next afternoon, white with scratches and dents in the paint, playing Metallica in the car and talking excitedly about the new cat her family just got. She hands me her phone to show me a picture. "Doesn't he look just like a raccoon? He's still super skittish, but he likes playing fetch." She offers me a drag of her clove cigarette, and I accept.

We get coffee before the movie, and in the coffeeshop she asks me about how I know Heather, about my favorite movies and books, about whether I've ever had Mr. Peterson, the English teacher who has a reputation for creeping on female students (I haven't). I ask her about the time Jack declared his love for her ("Your brother acts tough, but he bruises *super* easily, you know?") and what she's going to college for (physics) and how she got into LARP.

"James was the one who got us all into it. Sorry—does it bother you if I talk about James?"

"No, it's okay. I know you're all still friends with him."

"You're super pretty, by the way," she says matter-of-factly, and follows it up with, "I'm not flirting with you or anything. Just as a point of fact. Like, I love James and everything, but you're super gorgeous and nice and cool, and he let you get away, and that's just dumb."

"Wow. Thank you."

"Do you wanna be friends with him? Like eventually?"

"I don't know. Maybe."

"I think he wants to be friends with you. But you didn't hear it from me."

She shows me a drawing of the hawk tattoo she wants to get and asks if I want any tattoos.

"I used to talk with my ex–best friend about getting matching tattoos," I say. "We were gonna get little stars, like binary stars?"

"Oh my God, *don't do it*. My friend got one with her ex-boyfriend, and now she just has this dumb balloon tattoo that doesn't mean anything 'cause they broke up. Don't ever get a tattoo for someone else, trust me. I think I wanna get my hawk on my ribs so I can cover it with clothes and still look professional, you know? But I've heard that's *super* painful. Did you ever break a rib cheerleading?"

"No, but another girl did once." Lois, a senior girl my sophomore year. "Right in the middle of competition season, too. She probably should have taken more time off than she did."

"I feel like broken ribs are, like, the best injury to get 'cause you just kinda deal with it. But also maybe I don't know what I'm talking about."

We talk so much we miss the beginning of the movie, and after we sneak in late, I'm confused by the plot. It turns out not to matter. Every time there's blood on-screen, Andraleia and I shriek and hide our faces together. The acting and writing are ridiculously bad; sometimes we just rewhisper the lines to each other and laugh until we can't breathe. "I'm gonna make you bleeeeeeeeed," says the serial killer, and we can't stop repeating the line.

"I keep making friends with seniors," I say on the way home, trying to sound like I'm sort of joking. "You, Heather, my brother. You're all leaving."

She rolls up the window and turns down the music so we can hear each other better. "Well, I'm not going away for college."

"You're not?"

"Nope. I'm going to Mesa. Then hopefully UCLA, but we'll see."

"Oh. That's cool." I feel like crying with relief. And then I yell at myself in my head: *You guys literally just became friends a second ago. Why are you so happy?*

"Yeah, I had a health thing sophomore year that kinda shot my grades. I had to get surgery on these noncancerous tumors in my chest? So I ended up missing a whole bunch of school and community college first just made more sense. But I'm kinda glad. Took a lot of the pressure off."

"Sure, yeah."

When she drops me off, she hugs me good-bye across the front seat of the minivan, and then looks at me very seriously. "Jenna?"

"Yeah?"

"I'm gonna make you bleeeeeeeed!"

I laugh and pretend to rev a chain saw like the guy did in the movie. As soon as I get inside, I text her a little picture of a chain saw, and then immediately feel stupid. I've probably killed the joke.

But ten minutes later she's found a GIF of the guy saying the line and sent it back to me: *I'm gonna make you bleeeeeeed!*

I take a selfie of me making a face like the guy did in the movie and send it back. She sends me back a picture of her holding her cat like a chain saw, with just the word *BLEED* written on the image.

I hope you keep liking me.

Thirty-five

HEATHER TEXTS ME. I DON'T THINK WE'VE EVER texted each other before. I guess she got my number from the cheer contact sheet.

So great to see you last night! Lmk if you wanna be in the Coach tribute—rehearsals start next week. Either way see u at game. And a smiley emoji.

I start to text back: **Great to see u too! I don't think I'm gonna do it but ur awesome for thinking of me.**

But then I delete the second sentence and just send the first one.

I don't know why. It's not like I can even do the tribute. For one, I'm totally out of shape. For another, Raejean would shoot me on sight. So would the whole team, for that matter. I'm not gonna do it. But I decide not to say that straight-out and just let Heather figure it out. I don't want her to feel like I'm rejecting *her*.

I text again: **You and Adam are such a cute couple.**

Shit, was that too much? I panic for a second. But she responds right away:

Thank you! I think so too :-)

———————

For the next three days, I continue to think of arguments against doing Coach's tribute. *I'd just screw it up. Heather is the only one who even wants me there. I don't actually think she wants me there. She was just being nice. If Coach wanted me there, she would've asked me herself. I can't do that to Raejean.*

"It just wouldn't be fair to anyone," I find myself telling Jack after dinner. I make sure Mom doesn't overhear, because I know she'd just tell me to do it. "Plus, then I'd have to see Raejean."

Jack shrugs. "It sounds like no one's really asking you to do it."

"No, they're not. Heather mentioned it, but she didn't *ask* me to do it."

"So why do you keep arguing about it if you don't want to do it?"

"I'm not arguing about it."

"You've literally spent like twenty minutes telling me why you can't do it."

"Yeah, but that's not *arguing*."

"Why are you even thinking about it at all?" And to this I am silent.

I keep composing texts to send Heather in my head.

Thought about it and decided not to do the tribute. Thx tho.

I can't do Coach's thing but best of luck w/ it!

Not gonna be able to make it work :-(

But I don't send any of them.

Instead, I pull out my phone and start composing a text to Raejean. **Hey, Heather mentioned Coach's thing, just letting you know I'm not gonna do it so don't worry**—and then I delete it. I sit there with my phone in my hand, staring at the wall.

Or what if I just did it?

I scoff at the idea, but I keep thinking. *What if I went ahead and did it?* Maybe Evelyn Rice would give me lots of stank face. Maybe no one would talk to me.

Maybe I'd get to do that lift where I hold someone up with my feet. Maybe I'd get back in shape.

Maybe Raejean would cut me down in front of everyone. Maybe I'd be terrible at the moves.

Maybe I'd get closer with Heather. Maybe I'd get to do some of her choreography.

Maybe Coach would appreciate it.

I stare at my phone again, and this time, after I type, I hit Send.

Hey, been a while. Wanna clear the air. Coffee sometime?

And Raejean's response is nearly immediate:

Sure. This weekend?

thirty-six

I SEE RAEJEAN WALKING IN FROM THE PARKING
lot before she sees me. She's dressed down, not much makeup, in a
windbreaker with ratty jeans. She still looks nice; she always looks
nice. I've seen her around school since quitting cheer, but mostly at
a distance; this is the most close-up I've seen her in a while. She
doesn't look as good with short hair as I'd assumed she would, and
I want to feel some kind of vindication in this, but it just makes
me sad. It's growing back, though. Her hair has always grown fast.
She's not walking with a limp or anything, which is a relief to me.

I can't believe it's been five months since San Luis Obispo.

I planned my outfit like it was a date, wanting to look good
but not like I was trying too hard, effortlessly radiant like
Raejean always seems to pull off. I settled on a white cap-sleeve
dress with black polka dots and beaded flats. I try not to think
about whether I made the right call. I've been here for fifteen

minutes, and I've got my latte in my hands already, having tried with all my might to avoid gulping the whole thing down.

She sees me at my table without changing her facial expression and walks toward me. I smile at her; what's the right smile for a moment like this? She doesn't smile back, just sits down across from me with a neutral "Hey."

"Hey," I say. "Good to see you."

"Yeah," she says. "You already ordered?"

"Yeah, I . . ." Shit. I should've waited for her. Shit.

"Okay. I'm gonna go get something." And she immediately heads to the counter.

Stupid. I should've waited and then offered to buy her coffee. Stupid, stupid . . .

Wait a minute.

I notice the tightness in my chest and my stomach, once the rule of my daily physical state, but I suddenly realize I haven't felt this way in at least a month, maybe longer.

I didn't miss it.

And then I realize I don't miss Raejean, either. I miss laughing with her, I miss feeling known by someone like that, but I don't want her back. It's not an angry realization. It's quiet, as neutral as her face when she sat down. A simple and silent release, the cutting of an invisible umbilical cord. *I don't need to be your friend. It's okay. I release you.*

I take a deep breath and repeat the thought to myself:

I release you.

The tightness in my stomach doesn't disappear, but it stops

feeling urgent. All I have to do today is apologize; that's it. I don't need anything from her.

I release you. I release you. I release you.

She sits down again, coffee cup in hand.

"Pumpkin spice latte?" I ask.

"I wish. They're out of season." She gives me a strange, closed-off smile. "So, hi."

"Hi," I say. "How's it going?"

"It's fine." She rolls her eyes. "Been trying to squeeze in college visits around all the other end-of-semester chaos. Blech."

"Yeah, I think we're doing most of ours over the summer."

"But then you don't get to see what it's like when it's actually in session."

"I know, just . . ." I shrug and try to be casual. "Summer's a better time for my mom."

She takes a long sip and doesn't say anything. "Where all are you looking?" I ask, trying to keep the conversation flowing.

"Lotta UCs. UCLA, UCSB, UC Berkeley, USC . . ."

"Staying close to home," I say. This is a change from the last time we talked about this, when all Raejean wanted was to get as far away as possible from her mom.

"Yeah. I just really like not having a winter. What about you?"

"I'm still deciding. I'll probably stay in-state, too." I don't want to tell her I've considered any of the same schools, don't want her to think I'd be following her.

She takes another slow sip of her drink, and there's silence. "So what are we doing here?" she asks, and I giggle self-consciously.

223

"Um . . ."

"I mean, I can shoot the shit all day, but I'm guessing that's not why—"

"No. It's not. Um." Okay, I guess this is when it happens. I sit up a little taller. "Raejean."

"Jenna."

"I want to participate in Coach's tribute thing, and I wanted to make sure that was okay with you. And I wanted to . . . apologize. For cutting off your hair, and accidentally breaking your ankle, and . . ."

"Being kind of awful?"

The words sting, but I look at her face, and I can tell she's not being mean. And I realize that she's actually just stating a fact: I was kind of awful. "Yeah," I say, trying to laugh a little, "being kind of awful."

She nods, her face blank, takes another sip of her drink. "Well, that was easy," she says.

"What was?"

"I thought I'd have to make you apologize. This is great. You did all the work for me."

I laugh. "Make me apologize, like . . . torture me?"

She shrugs. "If that's what it took."

She's smiling. This is good, although I can't help noticing that Raejean isn't apologizing back. That's okay; maybe she's about to. "And," I continue, "you don't have to accept my apology, and you don't have to forgive me. I just wanted you to know that I'm sorry, and make sure it's okay for me to do Coach's thing."

"I mean, I'm not your babysitter. You can do whatever you want."

"Okay. Um."

"You should do the tribute. It'd be shitty of you not to. After what you put Coach through this year."

"I know, just—"

"Like, do you think I'm like a delicate little flower that can't handle seeing you?"

"No," I say. "I just wanted to be . . . respectful."

She nods. She's thinking. The tightness in my stomach is getting even tighter, and I just keep repeating in my mind, *I release you, I release you, I release you* . . .

"So are you, like, okay?"

This wasn't what I was expecting at all. "What?" I ask.

"Just, the way you were acting earlier this year, I wondered if there was some, like, mental health thing or something."

Part of me wants to scream at her, *If you think I should be in a freaking institution, just say so*, but there's genuine concern in her eyes. Who knows? Maybe there is a "mental health thing." Maybe I should ask my therapist brother. I breathe and try not to let on how much her words hit me in the stomach. "I've . . . felt a lot better lately," I say.

"Good," she says. "I'm really glad to hear that." And I can tell that she means it.

"I mean," she continues, "you cut my hair off."

"I know."

"And dropped me onstage."

225

"By accident. You know that was an accident, right?"

"No, I know, but . . ." And I'm not sure she does believe me. "You made me slap you in the face. In front of everyone."

"I know. I'm sorry for all that."

"It was just like, *whoa*, you know? Like, I thought I knew you, like really well, and then I just suddenly felt like I didn't."

"Well that's how I felt, too!" I can feel my voice jumping out of me, and I try not to shout. "Like, all of a sudden you didn't want to be around me, didn't want to even text me back half the time. How was I supposed to act normal when you just suddenly ditched me?"

"I only ditched you because you were acting weird," she says.

"I was only acting weird because you ditched me!"

Raejean looks down at the table, not meeting my gaze. "I don't think it happened like you think it happened," she says, calm.

And maybe she's right. Maybe my memory is playing tricks on me, and I was the weird one first. But I can't let it go.

"I mean, I felt like, when you started hanging out with Meghan all the time, I mean— You Mikey-Walled her German exchange student right in front of me—" And at this Raejean laughs a little bit. "What?"

"Using *Mikey Wall* as a verb. That's just funny."

"That's totally what it was, though."

"No, you're right. I did feel kinda bad about that."

"So I felt like I'd been traded in."

"Yeah, I know." She looks at her hands. "Meghan was just

really chill at a time when you were being decidedly . . . not chill. I dunno. Meghan's *fun*; you can't deny that Meghan is fun."

"I know. I like Meghan."

"Do you really?"

"I really do! I never had anything against her! I just . . ." And I trail off, stopping myself before I say *I just hated that you chose her over me.* Her faraway look makes me feel like she never saw me at all, like to her I'm just this vindictive weirdo with no chill, and the thought makes my chest hurt. "Was this all because of the water thing?" She looks up at me, confused. "Billy's birthday party. When I dumped the glass of water on your head?"

She thinks for a moment, then smiles. "Oh my God," she laughs. "I'd forgotten all about that. Wait, why did you pour water on me?"

"Because," I say, and my voice gets small, "you called me a ditz, and I hate it when you do that."

Raejean nods. She clearly hadn't thought about this before. "Sorry," she says, and I shrug. "I didn't know you hated it so much."

"I didn't at first," I said.

"I thought that's just what we do. We call each other names and we don't mean it and it's fine."

"It seemed like you did mean it."

"I didn't."

"Well. Thanks."

"You're really smart, Jenna. You're cuckoo for Cocoa Puffs, but no one can say you're not smart. That's why I called you a ditz, because it's so obviously not true."

"Thank you. Um. Please don't call me cuckoo, though?"

"Sorry."

"It's okay."

We sit in silence for a moment. She laughs to herself. "You dumped a glass of water on my head."

"Yup."

"I can't believe I forgot about that."

We sit in silence. I think I'm blushing, but the silence is okay.

"So how *is* Marcus?" I finally ask.

She laughs. "Marcus is an idiot," she says. "I think he expected American girls to be easy. I guess that's our reputation abroad? He got really confused when I wanted him to leave me alone."

"That sucks."

"It's whatever." She wiggles her eyebrows at me, a mischievous gleam in her eye that I haven't seen in months. "What about you? How's your love life?"

"Uh, nonexistent right now. I dated one of my brother's friends for like a second, but it didn't last . . ."

"Wait." She sets her coffee cup down. "Oh my God, which one?"

"Um. James."

"Wait, which one is James?"

"Um. You probably know him as Gemma?"

She thinks, then her jaw drops. "That quiet butch chick?"

"He's not a chick. He's transgender."

"Wait. You went out with a girl?"

"No, I went out with a transgender guy."

"Jenna, are you bi? Or gay? Because honestly that would explain so much."

"James is a guy. James is a guy. Going out with a guy does not make me bi or gay." I don't mean for it to come out as loud as it does. She throws her hands up in a kind of *my bad* gesture.

"It's nothing to be ashamed of if you are," she says.

"I know. It's just. He's a guy. He identifies as a guy, so he's a guy. He's gonna transition, and . . ." I let my voice trail off. I sound defensive and stupid.

"I guess I just don't know much about it," she says.

"Yeah, I mean, I didn't, either." I sigh. "I don't know what I am. I might be . . . something. I just know that I really liked him."

She nods. "Well. That's cool."

"Yeah, except he kinda broke my heart."

"Oh. That's . . . not so cool."

"I'll live."

"Do I need to kick his ass?"

"No, he's got enough to deal with. But thanks."

And she smiles and nods, and I think to myself that I don't think we're ever going to be close again, and that's okay. And at the same moment I also think,

"It's really good to see you."

And I say it out loud, and I mean it. She smiles.

"It's good to see you, too," she says, and I can tell she means it, too. "How's your mom?"

We keep talking for another hour. I tell her about playing Vampire: The Masquerade, about getting closer with my brother; she fills me in on the Marcus drama, and the cheer drama, and the medical drama with her ankle. It's easy. It doesn't feel like old times, because back then we would never have let such a long time go by without knowing every detail of each other's lives, but it feels nice. Like sitting next to a favorite cousin at Thanksgiving.

She hugs me good-bye when we leave. "I'll see you at practice," she says.

"See you at practice," I reply.

I climb into my car and just sit with my hands on the steering wheel. They're shaking a little. I don't think they were shaking five minutes ago, but they're shaking now.

I breathe deep and close my eyes, and I don't even know who I'm saying this to, but I whisper out loud over and over: "Thank you, thank you, thank you, thank you, thank you."

And when my hands have stopped shaking, I turn on the car and drive home.

thirty-seven

TOO LATE FOR ME TO DO COACH TRIBUTE THING?

Heather writes back right away: **No, not at all! R u in?**

Hell yeah! Let's do this!

She sends me a practice schedule—first practice is in a week and a half—and some instructional videos. There are three routines (one for alumni, one for the current team, and one for everyone), which will be interspersed between speeches about Coach. She also cautions me to keep quiet: Apparently this will come after the end-of-year dinner in May, which we do every year in the gym, but Coach has no idea that there will be any cheering, no clue about the scope of this tribute. When I realize that this is going to be a surprise, I cackle and cover my mouth; I cannot *wait* to see Coach's face.

Mom cries when I tell her I'm doing the tribute and hugs me for a really, really long time.

Heather and some other seniors have arranged for us to practice after school in secret locations so Coach doesn't suspect: a middle school gym, the auditorium, a dance studio downtown. When I show up to the first practice at the middle school, heart pounding, Heather greets me with a hug. "So glad to have you here!" I look around, and, to my relief, there are a number of girls I don't know, some of them noticeably older: alumni. The rest of the squad is mostly fawning over the alumni, asking about their colleges and careers—one of them apparently cheers for the Dallas Cowboys. A couple of girls say hi to me and "Welcome back"; Meghan even hugs me. Raejean gives me a smile and a wave from across the room. No one seems confused to see me; I guess Heather or Raejean must have given them a heads-up.

A few girls are chilly. Evelyn, Melissa, Becca. It stings, but soon I'm launching back into the moves. "Five, six, seven, eight!"

I've been stretching in my room for the past ten days, but my flexibility's still fallen off so much. I'll have to keep stretching basically nonstop. But I've been watching the instructional videos Heather sent me, and the moves are already partly in my body. It's definitely harder than it used to be, but it doesn't feel impossible. I wipe sweat off my forehead and try to jump higher.

Raejean is moving fine; I guess five months was enough time for her ankle to heal. She's not doing any big stunts, but she's hitting the moves with energy and precision.

Afterward, I see Heather sitting outside on a bench, engrossed in her phone. I tap her on the shoulder. "Hey, do you need a ride?"

"Oh, I am waiting for Adam, but thank you so much."

"Sure, no problem." I start to walk away and shout over my shoulder, "If you want one next time let me know!"

"Absolutely, thank you!"

At home, Jack makes fun of me for listening to the music tracks nonstop around the house, headphones permanently clamped to my head. "You're eating like a rabbit again," he laughs as I assemble a salad. I just roll my eyes at him.

The next time we practice, I can feel my muscles already adjusting to this new regimen; I can keep my balance and hold my leg up more easily. Raejean asks me to spot her as she practices her standing back tuck. One of the alumni compliments my form on my scorpion.

When Heather asks if I can give her that ride home today, I say yes and tell her in the car about the cheesy chain-saw movie I saw with Andraleia; she tells me about getting into UC Santa Barbara. "I have such senioritis now, it is so bad," she laughs. "I just want to sleep all the time."

"Are you staying in town for the summer?" I ask her. "I mean, not that UCSB's so far away . . ."

"Yes, I will be here," she says. "Working at a mall or something. Wherever will let me do things for money."

"I'll come visit you at the mall. So you don't get bored."

"Yes, please!" She adjusts her sunglasses and smiles. "Perhaps in an ice cream shop. Maybe I can get you free ice cream."

We hug good-bye outside her house, which isn't far from mine. "Thanks for the ride," she says.

"Anytime," I say. "Seriously, just let me know. You're not far from me, so it's no problem."

That night over teriyaki chicken, Mom asks, "Is the tribute thing open to the public?"

"Yeah, they're gonna have the audience come in when they put the music on and announce the surprise."

"Oh, right," Jack says, "Andraleia was saying she wanted to come."

I look up from my chicken. "Andraleia wants to come?!"

". . . Yeah? We were gonna go together?"

"Oh. Cool. Yeah, tell her to come."

"Seems like you and Andraleia have really gotten along," my mom says.

"Totally," I say. "She's great."

Later that night, I text Andraleia: **Hear ur coming to the cheer thing?**

She responds: **Hell yeah! Can't wait to see u in action!**

And then:

James wanted to come too but wasn't sure u wld be ok with it—is it ok if he texts u?

I read her words and can feel my pulse jump up in my neck, but I take a deep breath and respond:

Sure, thx.

And less than two minutes later, I have a text from James:

Hey. Hope ur good.

And then:

Heard about ur cheer tribute thing—u mind if I come see u do ur thing?

And then:

Jack and Andraleia said I could tag along

And:

So proud of u cheering again

And I respond:

Yes! Please come! And thank u :-)

And I add:

I know I was rly upset last time we talked but I would like to be your friend. If that's ok

And he responds:

I would like that too

And adds:

I'm sorry about all the things

And I reply:

I'm sorry too

And I send him the info. And I screenshot the conversation and send it to Jack even though he's in his room right across the hall. And he writes back, **Good.**

And I keep going to secret practices. And I keep giving Heather a ride home, sometimes blasting music, sometimes turning the stereo off to talk about cheer and game and guys and everything. And I keep getting better at the moves.

And I send Coach an e-mail, the most carefully worded

e-mail of my life, so as not to give anything away, but also so I don't have to find the words on the night of the tribute:

Hey Coach. Just wanted you to know that I wanna come back next year after all. Not sure if I'll have to try out again or anything but I'll do whatever it takes. Really sad that you won't be here for my senior year.

I made amends with Raejean. Maybe you already know that, I don't know. It was the scariest thing I've ever done but really really worth it. I don't know if we'll ever be close again, but I think we'll get along.

Since I left the team, I've gotten into my brother's hobby of Live-Action Role Playing, which is fun. Maybe Heather's mentioned that we've seen each other there?

Things were pretty awful for a while but then they were OK. I guess that's just life or whatever.

I just want you to know that it won't be the same without you and I can't thank you enough for being such an awesome coach. I'm sure I speak for everyone when I say we are going to miss the heck out of you.

And I also want to say I'm sorry. For everything. For every time I was late for practice, every time I didn't give it my all, and especially for all the ways I screwed up this year. I'm so, so sorry. With all my heart, I am sorry.

And I hope your wife will be OK. So sorry to hear about her mother.

Love,

Jenna

The next day, I get her response:

Attagirl.

I had a feeling you'd land on your feet. As much as I wish we could've had you on the team for competition season, as much as I would've liked to say good-bye to the team on a stronger year, I hoped—and believed—that you'd be fine. I'm glad to hear I was correct.

You feel things with your whole heart, Jenna, and that's actually why I didn't worry about you more. (That, and I know that your mom's a good egg.) The girls I have to worry about are the girls who push everything down and pretend their feelings aren't happening. If you can just get a little perspective as you get older, you'll be fine.

I appreciate that you're sorry, though it's really to your teammates that you owe that apology. I've no doubt that you'll figure out how to make it up to them when you rejoin the team. It sounds like you've done a lot of reflecting this year, which I'm glad to hear.

If you'd like, you're welcome to come to the end-of-year dinner—one last hurrah. I'd be happy to have you there. Details are below.

(The tribute—ha! She doesn't suspect a thing.)

Thanks for the wishes re: my mother-in-law. It's a big change and we are dealing with it one day at a time. If you ever find yourself in Berkeley, you've got a place to stay.

With so much love,

Coach

I cry when I read it. I take my laptop out to the living room and show Mom, and *she* cries. And when we've both blown our noses and calmed down, she grins and whispers, "I don't think she suspects anything about the tribute," and then she winks.

I whisper back, "I don't, either."

thirty-eight

AT THE END-OF-YEAR DINNER BEFORE THE TRIBUTE,
the other girls and I make a point of acting like we haven't seen
each other since I left the team, in order to throw Coach off. "Oh
my Gawd! How have you *been*?" We hug and air-kiss. We replay
"catching-up" conversations that we've already had.

Usually we all dress up for the final dinner, which presented
a problem: How would we do the routines if we're all in fancy
dresses? Ebony apparently proposed to Coach that we do the
final dinner in our uniforms: "It's the last time you'll get to see
us in them, Coach!" It was a risky move, but apparently Coach
didn't seem suspicious at the suggestion.

I haven't worn my uniform in so long—more than six
months. My belly and thighs are a tiny bit fuller than they used
to be, but I don't mind; it makes me feel more grown-up.

When I see Coach, I throw my arms around her, and she

laughs her deep-throated laugh. "Hey, kiddo. So good to have you back."

"Good to be here," I say, and I feel my heart twinge at the thought of not having her here next year.

The dinner proceeds as it usually does: folding tables with white plastic tablecloths in the middle of the gym, potluck dishes passed around, excited chatter that borders on shouting, sparkling cider in plastic champagne flutes. Heather and I chat quietly in our own corner. Raejean, at one point, mimes with her glass of water like she's going to pour it over my head, and at first I'm pissed, but then we both start laughing so hard I'm worried that I'm going to choke.

Coach raises her glass of sparkling cider and gives a toast. "It wasn't the year where we won the most competitions," she says, "but it was the year where I most saw the grit and determination of this team. Where I most saw you roll with the punches and step it up. So ultimately, yeah, I do think it was one of our best years. And I couldn't be more honored." I hang my head as she speaks, because I know none of this applies to me, but I applaud just like everyone else.

Per usual, Coach gives out awards: Team Player, Most Improved. The Couldn't Do It Without You award goes to Heather, who blushes and beams. Coach gives Raejean a new award she's never done before, the Never Give Up award, and we all rise to our feet for a standing ovation. Evelyn Rice shoots me a dirty look during the ovation, and I just smile back at her.

"And, Coach," Jodi says with a smile, "we got you an award, too." She runs behind the bleachers and retrieves a big bouquet of roses, with a card signed by all of us, and a certificate that reads *BEST F***ING COACH EVER*. "We just wanted to thank you so much for all these years of pushing us to be our best, and believing in us when we didn't always believe in ourselves, and . . ."

Coach is smiling, with this look in her eyes that says *Stop talking before I start crying*, but we all toast her with our sparkling cider, and she nods and nods. "Thank you, girls," she keeps saying. "Thank you."

"And," Meghan says, smiling, "there's just one more thing . . ."

She and Raejean nod to each other, run to the doors of the gym, and fling them open; a crowd floods in, parents and friends and faculty who had all been waiting in the parking lot this whole time, decked out in purple and yellow school spirit, while bass-heavy rhythmic music blares. And cheerleaders whisk the tables and food away in a blur of choreographed movement, as Coach's tiny wife, Julianne, grabs Coach's hand and escorts her to a seat on the bleachers. As a coterie of alumni come center court with a microphone, we all join them, and the music fades out.

"Hello, Coach," says Annie, the Dallas Cowboys cheerleader.

We look at Coach and see that her hands are over her mouth, tears streaming down her face.

"We heard you were moving on," Annie continues, "and we wanted to make sure to be here to give you the send-off you deserve.

241

"I'm Annie Tapper, class of 2013. I think I recognize some of y'all." Some people in the bleachers cheer. "I'm a cheerleader for the Dallas Cowboys now." More cheering. "My dream job. I can safely say I would never be doing that if it weren't for Coach. But what you taught me, what you continue to teach these girls, is so much more than cheerleading."

"You teach us resilience," Raejean says into another microphone.

"Respect," says another alum.

"Collaboration."

"Love."

"Dedication."

"Strength," I say.

"Joy."

"Teamwork."

"Coach Mason, you quite literally taught us to fly. And for that, we can never thank you enough."

And the crowd erupts in applause and screams. And I look past Coach's crying face, trying to find my mom.

There she is, recording everything on her phone, smiling ear to ear. Next to her is Jack, in his black sweatshirt and black jeans; Andraleia, clapping excitedly, making the sleeves of her flowy burgundy top wave like running water; and James, with his bow tie and suspenders, frantically shaking a purple-and-yellow pom-pom. He waves at me, smiling; I smile back.

"And to demonstrate our appreciation," Meghan says into a mic, "we're going to show you a little something we threw together." And the crowd loses it again.

As the microphones are taken offstage and we make our way into formation, I sneak a look at Heather, glowing and beaming, and she catches my eye and smiles wider;

and I look at Raejean, skipping with ease on her right foot, and she doesn't see me looking, but I can see that she is every bit as lit up as I feel;

and I look at Coach, her face full of pride and shock and grief and joy, squeezing Julianne's hand as she tries to stop crying;

and I look up at my mom and my brother and my friends, cheering and clapping for me in the bleachers;

and I don't know what's going to happen next year, when Heather and James and Andraleia and Jack all go to college, but I know that I'll be a cheerleader who does LARP and writes vampire stories and freaks out about things and crashes and bounces back, and that that's all basically fine;

and I look at my new squad in the bleachers, and my old squad around me on the floor of the gym, and I hit my position in the formation;

and for just a moment, in the silence before the music, I feel like I'm two people, the scared bundle of raw nerves who always thinks she's screwing everything up, and the calm one who can breathe and remember that it's all gonna be okay, and the calm one hugs the bundle of nerves and tells her, "Good job";

and then my two selves merge, and I realize I can be both people at once;

and the music starts, and I feel it vibrating inside my body;

and in the split second before I fly into motion, I know that I have never felt so whole, so alive, so free, as I do in this moment;

and then I dance.

Acknowledgments

There are so many people without whom this book, or I, would not exist.

Mom and Dad: I wouldn't be a writer if not for you. I wouldn't have grown up convinced of my own brilliance if not for you. I love you. Thank you.

RJ Tolan: This book would literally not have happened without you. Had you and Graeme Gillis not believed so deeply in *Baby Mama* and invited me to do it at EST, had Linsay Firman not brought Joy Peskin to see the show (big thanks to you, too, Linsay!), had you not introduced me to Joy, had you not created a structure in which I could keep working on *Squad* consistently, this book simply WOULD. NOT. HAVE. HAPPENED. Thank you, thank you, thank you.

Speaking of which, Joy Peskin: Oh my God. You've spoiled me for other editors. Thank you for understanding this book.

Thank you for never ever giving me a note that missed the mark. Thank you for your loving enthusiasm, and for giving me so much agency as a writer. You have, sincerely, been one of the best parts of this writing process.

Katie Shea Boutillier: Thank you for offering to represent me within a day of my contacting you. Thank you for believing in this book wholly and immediately.

To my fellow writers who offered their keen insight along the writing journey while letting me witness the birth of their own gorgeous books, Alex Borinsky, Paul Cameron Hardy, and Josh Conkel: your beautiful energy is within these pages. I hope you can feel it.

My brother, Matt: I hope you can tell from the character of Jack how much I love you. Thank you for making my teenage years bearable.

My sister, Monica: Thank you for teaching me what strength is.

My beloved Leo: This book, as well as my life as I know it, would never have come to be if you hadn't come to be. Thank you for changing my life in the most wonderful way, just by existing. I love you with all my being.

Will and Jeff, I love you and remain forever grateful that we found each other. Thank you for taking such good care of my boy.

Monica Byrne, thank you for helping me not freak out about suddenly being a novelist, and for all your guidance about the publishing process. And, also, just for being awesome.

Thank you to Michael Kosen for introducing me to the world of LARP all those years ago, and for patiently consulting with me on the details of the game for this book.

Thank you to Sam Tucker and Ashley Lauren Rogers for your invaluable insights into young James.

Thank you to those who shared their cheerleading insights with me: Bryn Boice, Camille B. Atkinson, Erica McLaughlin, Nicole Cushman, LaToya Davis, and Ashley Jacobson. Thank you for helping me get my head around this world.

To my once-upon-a-time dance teacher, Lisa Traver Strickland: That dance competition life, as well as the way you nudged our best dancing out of us, is all over this book. Thank you for creating such a vivid memory in me of what it meant to be artistically expressed and always getting better.

To my high school drama and English teachers, Stacey Allen and Pamela Ramsey: Would. Not. Have. Survived. High. School. Without. You. You may never know how much you changed the course of my life. Thank you.

Patrick Shearer: Your loving support while I was writing this book was invaluable. Thank you.

Diana and Leta: Like, do I even have to say it? Thank you for being my support system, my chosen family. Thank you for believing in my genius as much as I believe in yours. You should get thanked in every piece of art I do.

Grandma Beverly: I feel you in my veins and in my spirit all the time. I wish you could have read this book.

To all the amazing consent educators in my life, but especially to Andy Izenson: Thank you for making positive consent practices such a natural part of my consciousness that I take them for granted now; it changed the writing of this book in ways I only really became aware of in retrospect.

To my Patreon supporters: Brian Altschul, Brady Amoonclark, Gyda Arber, Andie Arthur, Ashlie Atkinson, Margot Avery, Christian Baker, Allison Keane Barr, Travis Bedard, Kathleen Bennallack, Randi Berry, Derek Bever, Pete Boisvert, Will Bond, Steven Boyer, Hope Cartelli, Jody Christopherson, Casey Erin Clark, Stephanie Cox-Williams, Mary Cyn, Lois Dawson, Elizabeth DeBold, Beth Derochea, LeeAnn DiCicco, Brooke Ashley Eden, Alice Flanders, Kavita Gadani, Martha Goode, Veronica Hand, Olivia Henley, Dominique Hernandez, Stephen Heskett, Rob Hill, Amy Jo Jackson, Bob Jaffe, Mandy Kelsey, Adam La Faci, Charlotte Lang-Bush, Brandon Lee, Stanley Lee, Elyse Levesque, Virginia Logan, Robin Macias, Douglas Mac-Krell, Johanna (Annie) Mahon, Andy Mallett, Laura Mariani, Ashley Marinaccio, Jacquelyn Marolt, Dani Martineck, Jaime Martinez-Rivera, Emily Maskin, Andrew Massey, Caitlin McDonald, Emily McNeil, Lauren Miller, Nicki Miller, Erin Moncada, Mandy Moore, Lindy Nichols, Hye Yun Park, Mathieu Perron, Andrew Peters, Natalie Ann Piegari, Hannah Hessel Ratner, Kelsey Rauber, Kristine M. Reyes, Hugh Ryan, Madhuri Shekar, Scott Sickles, Jen Silverman, Maggie Smith, Robin Sokoloff, Alexis Spiegel, Stephen Spotswood, Kacey Anisa Stamats, Jon Stancato, Adam Szymkowicz, Anna Trachtman, Eleftheria Tsipidi, Kristen Vaughan, Kathleen Warnock, C.L.